WEEKLY READER BOOKS presents

# Alex Gets The Business

## A Novel by Joe Claro

Based on the Paramount Television Series
FAMILY TIES

Created by Gary David Goldberg

This book is a presentation of Weekly Reader Books.
Weekly Reader Books offers book clubs for children from preschool
through high school.
For further information write to:
**Weekly Reader Books,** 4343 Equity Drive, Columbus, Ohio 43228.

Published by arrangement with Avon Books

AVON BOOKS

A division of The Hearst Corporation
1790 Broadway
New York, NY 10019

Printed in the U.S.A.

Interior photos by Alan Dockery.

# Family Ties®

## Alex Gets
## The Business

# CHAPTER
# 1

*BANG!* The kitchen door slammed against the wall as Alex came charging into the room. His sister Jennifer had been on her way to the refrigerator when Alex made his entrance. Now she was flattened against the wall, trying to stay out of harm's way.

*CRASH!* Alex's books hit the kitchen table. As he turned to face the center of the room, his other sister, Mallory, carefully poked her head in from the hallway.

Alex planted both feet firmly on the floor, held his arms out above his head, and let out a sound. It might have been the victory cry of a bull elephant. Or maybe not. Maybe it was the sound of Alex in love with himself. Whatever it was, it was *loud*.

"WHOOO-EEE!" Alex screeched. His sisters

stared, Jennifer still plastered to the wall and Mallory ready to run back into the dining room if Alex proved to be dangerous.

"WHOOO-EEE!" Alex repeated. He lowered his arms and his voice and addressed the room. "Ladies, congratulate me!" he announced.

"Did the Dow-Jones break another record?" Jennifer asked, leaving the wall and sliding into a kitchen chair.

"The Dow-Jones!" he said incredulously. "A mere numerical phantom for the parochial who can't see beyond the stock exchange. Jennifer, what happened today is positively . . . *cosmic!*"

"A stock exchange in space?" Mallory asked, tentatively stepping into the kitchen and taking a seat next to Jennifer.

"Forget the stock exchange!" Alex shouted, "Forget the Dow-Jones! You're looking at a man whose life has just assumed its predestined form. A man who can finally hold his head high as he proudly walks in—"

"Alex," Jennifer interrupted, her chin resting in her hand, "tell us what happened, or I'm going to set fire to your books."

Alex looked around, as if to remind himself of where he was. He flipped a chair around and straddled it backward, pushing it up to the table.

"Jennifer," he said solemnly, "Mallory. Today, I am a man."

"Leave the room, Jennifer," Mallory said, springing out of her chair. "Alex! How dare you

2

discuss such things with a child in the room!"

Jennifer made a move that Alex interpreted as an attempt to land a right hook on Mallory's chin. He put an arm out to guide her back to her chair and smiled at Mallory.

"Don't be silly, Mal," he said. "It's nothing like that. I just meant that today I took my first major step toward what I've always wanted out of life."

Mallory stared blankly at him. Then she squinted and asked, "Can you get arrested for it?"

Alex ignored the question. "Today," he said, "I was accepted as a brother in Nu Alpha Mu."

This announcement was greeted with silence and two puzzled looks from his sisters. Finally, Jennifer said, "A society dedicated to the preservation of baby talk."

"Nu Alpha Mu!" Alex said, rising. "Don't you two know anything? Nu Alpha Mu is merely the most important fraternity on campus! Better than that, every one of its members is a B-major."

"But I thought you were an A student," Mallory said.

"I am, I am," he said impatiently. "B-major, Mal. *Business* major. It's a very well-known fraternity for business majors!"

Mallory looked away and stared at the far wall. She seemed to be deeply engrossed in some topic other than the one they were discussing.

"What's the matter, Mallory?" Alex asked.

"I'm trying to see if I can think of anything more boring than a fraternity full of business majors," she said.

"Boring!" Alex sputtered. He looked over at Jennifer for consolation. She shook her head in mock understanding.

"Some people," she said, suppressing a smile.

"Mallory, listen to me," Alex said. He was on his feet again. This was going to be a challenge. He held his arms out and put his hands on her shoulders.

"Nu Alpha Mu," he said slowly, "is a national fraternity. That means they have chapters at colleges all over the country. Each of these chapters is known for taking only—how can I put this modestly?—the elite, the cream of the crop."

"Are they all business majors?" she asked guardedly.

"Yes," he said, releasing his grip and beginning to pace around the room. "NAM is a special-interest frat. That means that every fraternity brother—not just on my campus but throughout the country, Mal—shares my interest in making it in the world of big business in a big way."

"Wow," Mallory mumbled as she opened the refrigerator and took out a pitcher of orange juice.

Alex turned his attention to Jennifer, but he continued to speak to the room.

"That isn't all," he said. "The graduates in NAM are all *former* B-majors!"

4

"Gee," Jennifer said quietly, once again resting her chin in her hand and trying not to yawn.

"Don't you see what that means?" Alex said excitedly. When he got no response, he went on. "It means, dear sisters of mine, that the membership rolls of NAM read like a *Who's Who in American Business*. And *that's* why everybody who wants to excel in business wants to get into NAM. You come out of college as a NAM brother, and you practically walk right into the boardroom of some major corporation."

"No kidding," Jennifer said, taking a carton of milk from the refrigerator.

"What's a boardroom?" Mallory asked as she examined her nails.

"Board of directors, Mallory," Alex said. "You know, the guys who run things. Now that I've been accepted by NAM, I can just about have my pick of big bucks when I get out of school."

He paused. Now he had explained everything, in terms even a child could understand. Now they knew why he was excited. Now he'd get the reaction he had been expecting.

"Well," Jennifer said, getting up from the chair to return the milk carton, "I guess some part of this is just going right over my head. It's probably a lot more exciting than I can realize, Alex. And I'm probably pleased for you."

"Me too," Mallory said. "Probably."

Alex gaped open-mouthed from one sister to the other as a car pulled into their driveway.

Mallory looked out the window.

"Hey!" she said brightly. "It's Mom and Dad."

Alex was still gaping when his father came in and smiled. "Elyse," he called over his shoulder, "they're all home."

"Oh, good," she answered from outside. "See what they'd like for dinner, Steven."

"Hi, Dad," Mallory said. "I'll have the roast pheasant."

"Me too," Jennifer said. "But hold the ketchup."

Steven smiled at them. Then he turned to Alex as Elyse came in.

"You're home early, aren't you, Alex?" he asked. He and Elyse waited for an explanation, but Alex just stared at them. His mouth was still hanging open.

"Is something wrong?" Elyse asked. "Did something happen at school?"

"No and yes," Mallory said.

"What do you mean?" Steven asked her.

"No, nothing's wrong," Mallory answered. "But yes, something did happen at school."

"Yeah," Jennifer said. "Alex was just telling us about it. He just found out that he's been accepted into Goo Gabba Goo or something."

"Nu Alpha Mu!" Alex said angrily, turning to take a glass from the cupboard. He turned the cold water on full-force and glared at it as it ran into the sink.

"Nu Alpha Mu?" Elyse said. "Isn't that one of

the fraternities at school?"

"Right," Mallory said. "And they take only B students."

"B-majors," Jennifer corrected her. "That's short for business majors," she explained to her parents.

"Oh," Steven said. Then, after a pause, he looked over at Alex and asked, "But isn't that good news?"

"Yes!" Alex snapped, holding the glass under the running water.

"In fact," Mallory said, "it's really terrific news. It's going to get Alex into any boardroom in the country. Or something like that."

"Alex," Elyse said, putting her arm around his shoulders, "what's bothering you? Wasn't NAM your first choice of fraternities?"

"Yes, it was," Alex said calmly. "That's why I was so excited when I got home. But you try giving these two some good news." He took a long swallow of water.

"Oh, come on, Alex," Mallory said. "Your news isn't exactly up there with putting a man on the moon, you know."

"Maybe it is to him," Steven said.

"Right," Alex said, encouraged. "Maybe it's the best thing that's ever happened to me."

"Well," Steven said, "that could be overstating it a bit. It is, after all, only a fraternity."

"No, Dad," Alex said, getting excited again. "It isn't just a fraternity. It's *the* fraternity for anyone who hopes to make it up the corporate ladder. NAM has graduates in practically every major corporation in America."

"Oh?" Steven said, looking past Alex at the wallpaper. "Well, that's—very nice."

"Mmm," Elyse added, nodding her head.

"Well," Jennifer said, heading out of the room with her glass of milk, "one thing is clear. Nothing went over my head before," Mallory quietly followed her out of the kitchen.

"What kind of a family is this?" Alex cried. "Don't you guys understand? Being in NAM means the doors will open for me! My life is all worked out now. There are no more question marks."

"Alex," Elyse said, "you know life is more than which boardrooms you're allowed into."

"I know that, Mom," Alex said. He paused, then added, "I know it's more than that. But it isn't *a lot* more."

Steven and Elyse sighed together as their son picked up his books and marched out of the room. They exchanged a silent glance of mutual sympathy.

Then Steven said, "Who are we to say? Maybe he'll find a boardroom with kitchen privileges."

# CHAPTER
# 2

The next morning, Alex gulped down his break-fast, said a series of rapid good-byes, and dashed out the door just as his girlfriend, Ellen, drove up. He tossed his books onto the back seat, slid into the car, and pulled the door shut.

"Good morning!" he sang. "And how is the world's loveliest lady this fine day?"

"Very good, thank you," Ellen said, smiling. "I guess I know how you are. Sorry I didn't call you back last night. I didn't get home from dance class until after midnight."

"That's what I figured," Alex said. "It's no big deal. I just wanted to share some great news with you—I've been accepted into NAM."

"I'm happy for you, Alex. Of course, I'm not surprised at the news," she said as she drove onto the highway. "You have a lot more to offer them than they have to offer you."

"Absolutely untrue," he said. "Nu Alpha Mu is the elite of fraternities, as far as I'm concerned. This membership is going to cut a path for me right up to the directorship of IBM . . . or something."

Ellen drove on without commenting. He looked over at her and asked, "What's the matter?"

"Nothing," she said, trying to sound as though she meant it.

"No," he said. "Something's bothering you. My guess is that it has something to do with the frat."

"Why do you say that?" Ellen asked, still looking only at the road.

"Oh, I don't know. Maybe it's just men's intuition. Maybe it's ESP. Or maybe—just maybe—it's the fact that you haven't once told me you'd like to see me accepted into NAM."

"I never said I wouldn't like it," she said.

"Do you have something against NAM?" he asked.

She looked at him, then quickly back at the road. "Let's say I'm not crazy about Nu Alpha Mu," she said.

"But why?" he asked earnestly.

She hesitated for several seconds. Then she said, "The frat is filled with future titans of industry, Alex. I know you see yourself as one of those titans someday. And I don't doubt that you'll make it. Still, those guys seem obsessed with business—and with making money."

"I don't understand," Alex said. "What's wrong with wanting to make money?"

"Nothing," she answered quickly. "I hope to make some myself someday. It's just that making money isn't *all* I want to do. And sometimes I think it is all that matters to the guys in NAM."

Alex sat back and thought about that for a few moments. Finally, he said, "Look, I think you're being silly. Sure they talk about business a lot. That's their major, for Pete's sake! I mean, I'm as interested in Keynesian economics as you are in nineteenth-century American literature. Why shouldn't I want to be with guys who care about it as much as I do.?"

Now it was her turn to think. She drove off the highway and stopped at a red light. "You're probably right," she said. "At least I can't think of any way to argue with what you say."

The light changed, and she turned onto the campus. She drove up to the social sciences building, where Alex had a class beginning in five minutes.

As he reached into the back seat for his books, she said, "Just don't forget something, Alex."

Kneeling on the front seat, he looked over at her and asked, "Don't forget what?"

"That you're still the same guy who wrote me that poem about walking in the rain. Poems

11

don't make money. But don't forget it."

He leaned forward and said, "I'm not ever going to forget that." She moved her head and kissed him.

"Gotta go!" he said. "I think I'm late already!" He left her car and trotted to his first class.

Two hours later, Alex walked from the social sciences building to the Nu Alpha Mu frat house. This would be his first visit to the house as a member—a brother to all those other NAMs scattered about the country who were also planning how to make their fortunes.

The thought put an extra bounce into Alex's step as he walked up to the front door. He reached over to ring the bell, then suddenly remembered there was no need to. He fished in his pocket for his bright new key and proudly unlocked the door and stepped inside.

He saw four frat brothers spread about the living room. Like Alex, all four of them wore suits and ties. Only one was not wearing a vest. Feeling very much at home, Alex tossed his key into the air, caught it, pocketed it, and stepped into the living room.

"Morning, Walt," he said. "Tim. Frank. Lee. I was on my way to a lab, and I thought I'd stop by and see who was around."

He dropped his books on a chair as the others returned his greeting. Then he filled an empty easy chair, working hard to suppress the grin that kept threatening to reveal how delighted he was.

Walt, the chapter's vice-president, stayed slouched on the sofa but spoke in a mock-serious tone. "On behalf of everyone here, and indeed on behalf of all our brothers throughout the universe, I welcome you as a new member of Nu Alpha Mu."

"Thanks," Alex said, letting the grin emerge in full flower.

Walt got up and walked over to him. "No kidding," he said. "Welcome." He held out his hand, and Alex grasped it in a handshake.

"I was really impressed with your hazing project," Walt said.

"Which project was that?" Lee asked. "Did you do the paper refuting all the arguments in *Das Kapital?*"

"No," Alex said. "That was Mike Abrams. I wish I had drawn that project."

"Why?" Tim asked. "You did a nifty job on the one you got. What was the title of the report again?"

Proudly, Alex answered, "Short-term Business Prospects for the Newly Developed Area Southwest of the Campus."

"Right!" Tim said eagerly. "I read it the other night. It was brilliant! And a real page-turner."

"Thank you," Alex said, trying to sound modest. "But I don't think it was my best work. When the hazing committee posted the projects, I was

13

sure I could have done better with the attack on the unemployment insurance program. But you have to take what you get, I guess."

"Right you are," Frank said. "And your report *was* good. Even Simons thought so."

"Simons?" Alex asked. "You mean Professor Simons?"

"Yeah," Walt said. "As our faculty advisor, he gets to read all the hazing projects. He says it helps him keep tabs on the best students. I think he has your name written down on his hot prospects list."

Alex beamed. Simons was the only teacher he had ever looked at as an idol. Simons knew economic theory the way most people knew the inside of their homes. And he was the best teacher Alex had ever come across.

When the hall clock chimed, Alex jumped up from his chair and grabbed his books.

"Gotta go, guys," he said. "Class in ten minutes."

He raced out of the frat house, turned in the direction of the lab building, and stopped short when he heard a female voice calling his name. He turned and saw Nan Winters rushing to catch up with him.

Alex was a little puzzled at why Nan might want to see him. They were in Simons's eco class together, and although they traded an occasional hello, Alex hadn't thought that she even knew his name.

Alex just wrote this off to the fact that she was stunningly pretty, and therefore probably exercised a great deal of discretion in deciding which males she would allow to talk to her. But here she was, running to catch up with him.

"Alex," she said, a little short of breath, "I'm so glad to see you. I heard last night about your acceptance into NAM. Congratulations."

"Thanks," Alex said. He suddenly forgot about being late for his lab class. As he looked at Nan's sparkling green eyes, he realized that they might almost be as beautiful as freshly minted ten-dollar bills.

"Nu Alpha Mu is my favorite fraternity," Nan said. "Always has been. A lot of guys in NAM are good friends of mine."

"Really," Alex said, almost stammering. "Well, I—I just didn't know that."

"Now that you're in the frat," she went on, "I hope you'll be a friend of mine too."

"Well, yeah," Alex said, unable to stop staring into her eyes. "I mean, sure! I'd like that very much!"

"Good," she said, giving him a broad smile. "I have a lot of respect for anyone who can make it into Nu Alpha Mu. I know what they require of you. I know how high their standards are. So I know that if they took you, then you must be someone I can respect."

Alex felt giddy, and he was once again faced with the problem of suppressing a silly grin. Was

she really talking to him? She had said something about respect, hadn't she? And something
about being friends?

And now wasn't it his turn to say something?
Isn't that the way conversation works? he heard
himself thinking.

"Uh—thanks," he said lamely.

"Sure," she said. "I have to rush. Glad I ran
into you." And she headed back the way she had
come.

Alex let the grin break through. Wow, he
thought, life is wonderful. Not only do I make
Nu Alpha Mu fraternity, my ticket to the big
time, but Nan Winters, Miss Beauty and Brains,
wants to be my friend.

He nearly skipped to the lab building.

# CHAPTER
# 3

"Now, remember," Professor Simons told the class, "you have a paper due on a comparison between the causes of the depression in the U.S. and in Germany in the 1930s. It's due next Thursday, and I won't accept any excuses for lateness."

He paused and looked over the students in his economics class. "Any questions?" he asked. Most of the students, Alex included, were already packing their books, getting ready to leave.

"All right, then," he said pleasantly. "I'll see you all on Tuesday."

A low murmur of conversation began, joined by the scraping of a few chairs along the floor. Alex made his way toward the door, together with the rest of class.

"Oh, Alex," Simons said. "If you have a minute, I'd like to talk to you."

Alex noticed several of his classmates turning to look at him. He did his best to appear cool, but he could feel his face turning red.

"Me?" he asked in a voice he tried to make sound casual, but which actually came out as a high-pitched squeak. "Oh, sure, Professor Simons. Sure I have a minute."

As he turned to face Simons, Alex caught his foot inside a chair leg. That threw him off balance and sent his books crashing to the floor. He bent down to retrieve the books, and two pens fell out of his shirt pocket.

He started scrambling to collect everything, then suddenly realized how ridiculous he must look. So he closed his eyes for a second, then stood up straight. He noticed with relief that everyone else was gone.

"Excuse me, Professor," he said. "Just give me a few seconds to pick this stuff up and start all over again. Very careless of someone to leave that chair in the middle of the aisle," he added lamely to cover his embarrassment.

Simons smiled as Alex bent down, picked up the pens and put them into his pocket, and collected his books. He stood, put the books down on a student desk, and said, "What did you want to talk to me about, sir?"

"First, about your report on the monetary system," Simons said. When Alex's eyes widened and his face began to fall, Simons added quickly, "It was excellent."

This time, Alex let the grin out without any hesitation. "Really?" he said. "You said excellent, didn't you?"

"Yes, I did," Simons said. "Though I'm not at all surprised. Everything you've done in this course is first-rate."

"Thank you, sir," Alex said, delighted at the compliment but disturbed because his voice came out in the kind of squeak usually associated with inhaling helium. "Thank you very much," he said more deeply, just to be sure Simons knew what his voice really sounded like.

"I don't know if you've decided on a more specific major yet, Alex," Simons said. "But I certainly hope that you're considering economics."

"Well, yes, sir, I am," Alex said. "Of course, I don't have to make my decision until next semester. But economics is still my first and only choice."

"Good," Simons said. "I'm going to do what I can to see that it remains so."

"I'm flattered, sir," Alex said.

"No need to be," Simons said, putting his books into his briefcase. "You have a lot to offer, Alex. As much potential as I've ever seen in a student."

Simons began moving toward the door, and Alex followed. "By the way," Simons said, "congratulations on your Nu Alpha Mu acceptance."

"Thank you again," Alex said. Then he wondered, how many times can a person say thank you in the space of a minute?

"When I was your age," Simons said as they walked toward the parking lot, "fraternities weren't held in very high regard. It was the late sixties, and it wasn't the 'in' thing to join a fraternity."

"Yeah, I know," Alex said. "My parents were in school at the same time. When they talk about Berkeley—"

"Did your parents go to Berkeley?" Simons asked. "That's where I did my undergraduate work."

"No kidding?" Alex said. "You know, you're about the same age as they are. Wouldn't it be something if you were at Berkeley at the same time?"

"Yes, it would," Simons said. They had reached his car, and he dug his keys out of his briefcase. "I'd like to meet your parents sometime," he said. "If they ever come to campus for some event or other, be sure to let me know. Maybe we can get together."

Suddenly Alex felt impulsive. "Why wait for a campus event?" he asked. "We'll create our own event. Why don't you come to the house for dinner? Say, sometime next week?"

"That's very nice of you," Simons said. "Do you think you should clear it with your parents first?"

"No need," Alex said. "I bring friends home for dinner all the time. That is, I didn't mean to imply that you and I are *friends*, Professor Simons. What I mean is, I think they'd love to have you over for dinner. Especially when they hear about Berkeley."

"Good," Simons said. "But I'd still like you to clear it with them. Next week—any night but Thursday will be fine."

"Great!" Alex said. "I'll talk to them tonight and let you know tomorrow. Oh, and by the way, Mrs. Simons is invited too, of course."

"There is no Mrs. Simons," he said, climbing into his car. "But I would like to bring a close friend, if that's all right with your parents."

"Sure thing," Alex said. He waved as Professor Simons pulled out of the parking space and drove off.

As he watched the car move away, Alex grinned once again. Professor Simons is coming to my house for dinner, he thought. Professor Theodore E. Simons, author of the award-winning *Economics: The Ultimate Reality*, is going to break bread with the Keatons.

21

He turned and began walking toward the frat house. Hmm, he thought. I hope they don't spend the whole night talking about Berkeley. I'll just have to take steps to see that that doesn't happen.

# CHAPTER
# 4

"Theodore Simons?" Elyse asked.

"That's right," Alex said. "He's my economics teacher."

She was standing at the counter, cutting melon into strips. "Why is that name familiar?" she asked.

"He's a well-known economist," Alex said. "He's written half a dozen textbooks."

"No," Elyse said, shaking her head. "Writing an economics textbook doesn't get anyone into my private pantheon of celebrities."

"Maybe you saw him on TV," Steven said. He was at the sink peeling potatoes. "In fact, it could have been on one of our programs," he added, referring to his job at a public TV station.

Elyse stopped her work and looked off into space. "You just might be right, Steven," she said. "One of those programs about economics. One of those interview programs. The kind I always find so difficult, so boring, so—"

"Of course, you might have seen him on the 'Today' show," Steven said. "And if you think those shows are boring, why do you watch them with me?"

She turned to face him. "I don't really think they're boring," she said, smiling. "It's just that sometimes, after a hard day at the drawing board, I need something a little more relaxing than the rise and fall of pork belly futures, or the causes of the current drop in the value of the dollar."

"A point well taken, Mom. There's nothing relaxing about the fall of the dollar, unless of course you've made a slight investment in the Japanese yen," said Alex with a big smile, indicating that he had done just that. He opened the refrigerator, took out a carrot, and bit off a chunk. "Just remember though," he added, "some people feel about architects the way you feel about economists."

"Not economists," she said. "Economics. And don't talk with your mouth full."

Steven finished with the potatoes. As he was washing his hands, he said, "In any case, Alex, did you say you've already invited this Professor Simons?"

"Yeah, Dad. I hope it's okay. I mean, he said he wanted to meet you guys, and it was a kind of spur-of-the-moment thing."

"Sure, it's okay," Steven said. "Why does he want to meet us?"

"Well, mainly, Dad, because he wants to meet the parents of such a brilliant student," Alex said as Mallory came into the kitchen. "He did his undergraduate work at Berkeley. He's about your age, so he must have been there the same time you guys were."

"What's this?" Mallory asked. "Who went to Berkeley?"

"Professor Simons, my economics teacher. I've invited him for dinner next week."

"You've invited somebody who went to Berkeley during the sixties? Alex, don't you have any control over your behavior? Don't you realize what you've done?"

"What are you talking about, Mallory?" Elyse asked. She covered the bowl of fruit and slid it onto a rack in the refrigerator. Then she turned to face Mallory. "What has he done?" she asked.

"Oh, come on, Mom. You know how you and Dad get whenever you get together with someone from your past. You'll be singing those Peter, Paul, and Mary songs, and talking about the Peace Corps and dropping out, and—and—I'll have to listen to the original cast recording of *Hair* all the way through again!"

Elyse walked over and put her arm around Mallory, who was almost in tears. "Take it easy, dear," she said. "You really do have a tough time of it, Mallory. I just don't know how you put up with us."

"Tell you what," Steven said, sitting at the

kitchen table. "I'll make you one promise. No matter what happens, we won't play the *Hair* record. Fair enough?"

"I guess so," Mallory said, sitting opposite him at the table. Then she looked over at Alex and asked, "Did you say this is one of your teachers?"

"Yep. My economics professor." Mallory looked blankly at him. "Economics, Mallory," he said. "It's the science of the production and consumption of wealth."

"Really?" she asked, raising her eyebrows. "Is this man very wealthy?"

"No," Alex said, annoyed, "he isn't very wealthy."

"Mustn't be a very good scientist, then," she said.

"I took one eco course in college," Steven said loudly, trying to shift the subject a bit. "And I tell you, it was probably the hardest course I ever took with the possible exception of physics."

"I never could understand why you had so much trouble with that course, Steven," Elyse said.

"It had something to do with attitudes," Steven said. "I could never understand how anyone could devote so much attention to— well, money."

"No, Dad," Alex said. "It isn't just money. Economics deals with anything that contributes to the wealth of nations. There's supply and demand, labor, natural resources, sociological factors, and on and on. All these things work together in an intricate system that results in the production, distribution, and consumption of wealth."

Steven was staring glassy-eyed at his son. "Like I said," he muttered, "money."

"Well," Elyse said, "I'm sure we'll have plenty of things to talk with Professor Simons about other than money."

"Professor who?" Jennifer asked as she came in through the back door.

"Professor Simons," Alex said. "He's—"

"An economics teacher," Mallory said. "That's the science of wealth, but he isn't wealthy, not even a little bit. He teaches at Alex's school, and he's coming here for dinner next week. And wait, you haven't heard the best part. He went to Berkeley at the same time as Mom and Dad."

"Berkeley!" Jennifer said, horrified. "That means 'The Age of Aquarius' and 'If I Had A Hammer' all night long!"

"No," Alex said. "That's already been taken care of. Dad has promised no cast recording of *Hair* or Peter, Paul, and Mary for the whole night."

"Oh," Jennifer said, relieved. "Did Mallory say this guy is one of your teachers?"

"Right," Alex said.

"Didn't you have one of your high school teachers here for dinner once?" she asked.

"It was elementary school," he answered, "and

you were too young to be able to remember it now."

"Yeah, but I've heard about it," Jennifer said meaningfully. "What was her name again?"

"Her name was Miss Maywood, and she was very fond of Alex," Steven said.

"As I remember it," Mallory said, "it was Alex who was very fond of her. Madly in love with her, if I'm not mistaken."

"Alex did have something of a crush on Miss Maywood," Elyse said. "But so what? She was a very nice young woman, and we had an enjoyable evening together."

Alex said, "Enjoyable if you forget that I spilled ice cream on her dress, broke the heel off one of her shoes, and nearly set her on fire when I knocked the lamp over."

"Yes," Steven said. "Well, you were nervous. It was an awkward situation."

"Right," Alex said, forgetting about Miss Maywood's visit. "And, Jennifer, that doesn't have anything to do with this. Professor Simons is a nationally known economist, lecturer, and author. He also happens to be the faculty advisor to Nu Alpha Mu, and one of the nicest teachers I've ever had."

"Are we going to have to applaud when he comes in?" Jennifer asked.

"No, Jennifer," Alex answered. "Just try to remember your manners and to keep Mallory from saying anything too stupid."

"Alex," Mallory said, "the only one around here who ever says anything stupid—"

"That's enough," Steven said, getting up from his chair. "Jennifer and Mallory, go set the table for dinner. Alex, give me a hand with the burgers."

Mallory glared at Alex. Then she and Jennifer went to the dining room.

"Is Professor Simons bringing his wife to dinner, Alex?" Elyse asked.

"He isn't married," Alex said. "But he said he'd like to bring a date."

Mallory called out from the dining room, "Let's hope she didn't go to Berkeley too!"

# CHAPTER
# 5

"Which way are you going, Alex?" Nan asked as they left their management class.

"Huh?" Alex said, turning to see who was talking. "Oh, Nan. I didn't see you. I'm going to the frat house."

Actually, he had seen her out of the corner of his eye and had just pretended to be unaware of her. He was still sure about his love for Ellen, but he also knew that Nan's attentions toward him were not exactly unwelcome. Having a beautiful, intelligent young woman interested in him was not exactly unflattering.

Alex decided to come on as cool as possible until he found out if she were really interested in him. If she were, then—well, I'll let her down gently, he thought.

"I'll walk with you," Nan said. "I'm on my way to the library."

"Oh, Nan," Alex said, holding the door so she

could step outside before him, "the library is in the opposite direction."

She turned and smiled at him as he followed her out the door. He looked at her smile and suddenly realized what it would feel like to have knees made of Jell-O.

They walked along a tree-lined path, and Alex desperately tried to think of something to say. Nan saved him by asking a question.

"Did you watch the debate on inflation last night?"

"No," Alex said nervously. "No, I didn't. I had already seen the program, in fact."

"But it wasn't a rerun," Nan said, puzzled.

"No, it wasn't," Alex said, trying not to look at her eyes for too long at a stretch. "I got to see the program in advance."

"Really?" she said. Since she sounded impressed, Alex began to lose some of his nervousness.

"Yeah," he said. "My father is the station manager at WKS. He brings home tapes a lot. Usually, they're about animals facing extinction, or ballet companies from Siam, or something like that. But every once in a while, he gets something worth watching."

"That sounds great," Nan said. "When did you see the program?"

"Some time last week," Alex said, trying to sound as though he took these advance screenings very casually. The fact was, he and his sisters got a huge kick out of seeing a program before it was aired, even if it was about Siamese ballet dancers.

"Do you ever work at the station yourself?" she asked.

"Oh, sure," he answered as they turned the corner next to the frat house. Now that he had her interest, he had lost his nervousness, and his voice was back to its normal pompous ring.

"Sure," he went on. "I've worked in the control room with the directors, and I've been out on shoots for one or two news reports."

He figured it wasn't necessary to point out that his visit to the control room had taken place when he was eight years old. Or that he had been asked to go out with the news crews so they'd have someone to go and buy lunch for them.

"That must be very exciting," Nan said. They stopped walking at the frat house entrance, and she leaned against the fence, obviously in no hurry to get wherever she was going. "Do you hope to go into that field someday?"

"Not a chance," he said. "My interest is in business. Maybe corporate law. Or possibly international finance. Working at a local TV station just wouldn't cut the mustard, I'm afraid."

"I see what you mean," she said, giving him another intimate smile. This one caused his toes to turn into French fries. "I don't think it matters much what you choose to do, though," she added.

"What do you mean?" Alex asked.

"I have the feeling you'll be a smashing success at anything you pick," she said.

She wasn't smiling now. In fact, she was looking very serious, as though she wanted to underline the importance of what she had just told him. He could feel his elbows beginning to tingle.

"Gee, thanks," he said weakly, staring into her eyes. Now a new thing was added to the physical sensations, a sound that made it hard for him to think. Was it an alarm of some kind? A trumpet? A car horn?

*A car horn.* He turned to see Ellen's car waiting at the curb. As she looked at him, Ellen gave the horn two more short beeps.

"Oh, there's my ride home," Alex said as his face turned red. "I have to go, Nan. It was nice talking with you."

He backed away and gave her a small wave of his hand. She responded with a huge smile and a wave to match.

"Even nicer talking to you, Alex," she said loudly. "I'll see you tomorrow."

Had Ellen heard that? Alex wondered. He hurried to the car, got in, leaned over, and kissed her on the cheek. "How you doing?" he said casually.

"Fine," she said as she eased away from the curb. "Who was that?"

"Who?" Alex said. "Oh, you mean her. A girl. She's in a couple of my classes."

"What's her name?"

"Her name?" Alex said, as though he had just been asked to recite the entire encyclopedia. "Her name's Nan. Why do you want to know that?"

Ellen looked over at him. Were her eyes crinkling up into a smile? "No reason," she said. "She's pretty."

"Yeah," Alex said too quickly. "I mean, I guess she's pretty."

He looked over at her and studied Ellen's profile. The angle of her cheekbones had always been the part of Ellen's face that he liked best. He also liked the slight imperfection at the top of her nose, one of the few flaws that made Ellen look like a mere mortal.

She looked straight at the road, so he couldn't see her eyes. But he knew what they looked like. He thought about how they always reminded him of deep pools of water at dusk. He thought, too, about her smile, that 250-watt special event that always stopped him dead in his tracks.

Then he thought about his conversation with Nan and felt queasy.

"She's only pretty," he said. "You're beautiful."

She turned to face him. She was wearing the half-smile, half-smirk that was her standard response to his comments about her beauty. She had decided years earlier not to say anything to such comments. Not even thank you, which would imply that she had something to do with being beautiful. She realized that most people found her very attractive, but she didn't want that fact to be important to her or her relationships.

"I can't make it for dinner next Tuesday," she said. "I'm sorry."

"Oh, that's too bad," Alex said. "I really wanted you to meet Professor Simons."

"I was looking forward to it too," she said. "But my bio teacher offered some extra lab time on Tuesday afternoon. He said he'd help us out with anything that's giving us trouble. In my case, that's almost the whole course."

"Tuesday afternoon?" Alex said hopefully. "But we're not having dinner until seven-thirty. You'll be able to make it."

"No," she said. "In order to take the lab, I had to switch my dance rehearsal. So I won't be finished until about ten."

"Well, maybe next time," Alex said gloomily, staring out the window.

"Sorry, Alex," she said. "I would have enjoyed it."

"It's okay," he said.

He wasn't thinking so much about his disappointment at her not being able to come. He was thinking—or trying to think—of just how this tied in with the conversation he had been having with Nan when Ellen showed up.

How could it tie in? he wondered. The two things had nothing to do with each other. But they did, he thought. Somehow, he had done something to deserve this disappointing news. They were definitely related.

It was a totally new experience for Alex. He was learning firsthand what other people meant when they talked about guilt feelings.

# CHAPTER

# 6

"Mallory," Alex said the following Tuesday night, "did you check to see if they're here yet?"

Mallory was sitting on the couch, reading a magazine. "Yes," she said without looking up at him.

"How long ago?" he demanded.

Still keeping her eyes on the magazine, she said, "About thirty seconds. That was the last time you asked me to check."

Exasperated, Alex turned to Jennifer, who was looking through the record cabinet. "Jennifer!" he hissed. "Those shoes! Do you really think they're appropriate for the occasion?"

"The occasion is dinner, Alex," she said, thumbing through the records. "These shoes have been to dinner with me dozens of times before."

Alex busied himself primping up the room. He straightened a picture that didn't need straightening. Then he moved some magazines from one end of the coffee table to the other, thereby reversing an adjustment he had made two or three minutes earlier.

He was about to move one of the easy chairs to the other side of the room when Elyse and Steven came in, each carrying a tray of hors d'oeuvres. Alex stopped in his tracks and looked them over.

"Mom," he said, "maybe you want to tie your hair back in a bun. Dad, why don't you straighten your tie? Just put the trays on the coffee table, and I'll—"

"Shut up, Alex," Elyse said softly. She and Steven carried the trays to the coffee table and put them down.

"Mom, they'll be here any minute!" he said frantically.

"Alex," Elyse said, trying to check her annoyance without much success, "they're two normal human beings, not ambassadors from another planet."

"But, Mom—"

Steven stood in front of him and put his hands on Alex's shoulders. "Alex," he interrupted. "You're my son, and I love you. But your behavior today has gone beyond what anyone should have to put up with. Calm down. Get hold of yourself. If you can't then pretend. Otherwise, I might have to insist that you find your own apartment to move into. Tonight."

Alex opened his mouth to object. Steven held up a finger as a warning. Alex took a breath, closed his mouth, and threw himself on the couch at the opposite end from Mallory.

Jennifer got up from the record cabinet and walked to the stairway. She was carrying a record.

"What's that, Jennifer?" Elyse asked idly.

"Nothing," Jennifer mumbled and hurried toward the stairs.

"Jennifer?" Elyse said. "Why are you taking a record upstairs? There's no record player up there."

Jennifer stopped at the foot of the stairs. "I wasn't going to listen to it," she said. "I was going to hide it."

Elyse had walked over to her, took the record, and looked at the cover. *"Hair,"* she said. "But your father promised he wouldn't play this. You don't have to hide it."

"I thought he might weaken," Jennifer said. "I figured I'd remove the possible source of temptation."

"Don't worry," Steven said, smiling and taking the record from her. "I think I'll be able to resist any temptation that arises." He walked over to the record cabinet and slid the record back in while sneaking a fond glance at the album cover.

The front doorbell rang. Alex sprang from his seat and bolted toward the door, tripping on the step. When he reached the door, he turned to face his family. He gave them one last look of inspection, adjusted his jacket, and put his hand on the doorknob.

"Everybody ready?" he asked over his shoulder.

"Alex," Steven said, "just open the door, and try not to trip on the way down."

He swung the door open, and Professor Simons smiled and said, "Hello, Alex."

"Hello, Professor Simons," Alex said, suppressing the urge to bow. He stepped aside to allow Simons and the young woman with him to come inside.

Simons stood between her and Alex and said, "Marcie Sutton, this is Alex Keaton."

"How do you do, Alex," Marcie said, holding out her hand.

Alex, who wasn't in the habit of shaking hands with a woman, hesitated for a fraction of a second. Then he offered his own hand and said, "Pleased to meet you, Miss Sutton."

"Marcie," she said.

"Yes," Alex said. "Marcie." He held out his arm to include his family in the introductions. "This is my father, Mr. Steven J. Keaton," he said.

Steven stepped forward and shook hands with both guests. "I'm Steve in most situations," he said.

"And this," Alex said, "is my mother Elyse Keaton, formerly Elyse Donnelly."

"Of the Cleveland Donnellys," Elyse said, giving Alex a sidelong glance and shaking hands with them.

"And this is my sister Mallory, and my other sister Jennifer," Alex said.

Both girls nodded and said, "Hi."

"That's a terrific haircut, Jennifer," Marcie said. "Where did you get it?"

"Mallory cuts my hair," Jennifer said as everyone walked into the living room.

"Alex, why don't you do the honors and serve some refreshments," suggested Elyse.

Alex asked what everyone wanted to drink. Then he went into the kitchen.

Alex's absence from the room gave his sisters and parents a chance to get to know their guests without having to worry about how he was holding up under the strain. By the time he got back with the drinks, he was relieved to see that the conversation was moving along very smoothly, even without his guidance. He was happily surprised.

Alex sat in a chair, sipping his cola and only pretending to be part of the general conversation. He had caught only the tail end of Simons telling his parents what a good student their son was. Just as well, he thought. I would have had to do the fake modesty bit, and I'm never comfortable with *that* routine.

Now they were into Berkeley, and the crucial question was: *Will they succumb once again to nostalgia and thereby ruin the entire evening?*

41

Alex glanced at the clock and decided he would allow them exactly twenty minutes. If they were still on Berkeley and the sixties after that time, he would think of something to do to stop it. Break a window in the kitchen maybe, or get Jennifer to trip and hurt her ankle.

He half-listened to the conversation and half-thought about the time. Marcie was talking to Mallory and Jennifer about hair. To his surprise, Simons and his parents were not talking about *Hair*, or Berkeley, or the sixties. They were into some documentary that WKS had shown a couple of weeks ago.

Alex looked at the clock again. Less than ten minutes had gone by. Could they actually have exhausted their college days in so short a time? Unlikely, Alex decided. It would come up again. He'd have to remain vigilant.

"Dinner's all prepared," Steven said, getting up from the couch. "Elyse got everything ready ahead of time. I'll have it on the table in a few minutes."

"I'll give you a hand, Dad," Alex said, getting up and following him toward the kitchen.

"Thanks, Alex," Steven said. "I can handle it. Stay with the guests."

Alex decided that this would be a good opportunity to talk with Professor Simons in a relaxed atmosphere, to listen to his brilliant insights on economic matters. If this happened to help his grade average in school, so much the better.

Alex was just about to get the ball rolling when Marcie said, "Ted, I was just telling Jennifer and Mallory about my plans."

"You mean about your business?" Simons said, taking a sip of his drink.

"She's going to open a hairdressing shop, Mom," Mallory said.

"Really?" Elyse said. "That used to be a secret ambition of mine."

"It's been my ambition for years," Marcie said. "My bachelor's degree is in marketing, because even way back then I knew I wanted to have my own business."

"And she does haircuts and perms in her spare time," Simons said.

Steven came in and announced that dinner was served, and everyone moved to the dining room. Once they were all settled, Elyse said she wanted to hear more about Marcie's plans.

"Steven," she said, "Marcie is going to open a hairdressing shop."

"Well," Marcie said, "not just yet. I still need more capital than I have. I'm going to have to find an interested investor before I can get started."

Simons took a serving platter from Steven and put a slice of meat on his plate. He passed the platter to Marcie and said, "I've offered to be the investor Marcie needs. But she won't hear of it."

"No," Marcie said. "I'd rather keep my personal life out of my business dealings."

"You have a point there," Elyse said. "Mixing them could lead to trouble."

"Do you have any other offers?" Steven asked.

"Nothing solid," Marcie said. "I have a cousin who may be interested. Then again, she may not be."

"How much do you need?" Jennifer asked.

"Jennifer," Elyse said, "that isn't an appropriate question."

"Oh, that's all right," Marcie said. "I don't mind telling you. I brought the subject up in the first place. I'm short exactly ten thousand dollars, Jennifer."

"Wow!" Mallory said. "That's a lot of money!"

"Well, it's all relative, Mallory," Steven said. "Though I can say that no relative of mine is going to be able to help you, Marcie."

"Dad," Jennifer said, "that was a terrible joke."

"I know," Steven said, "but I just couldn't resist. Besides, it's true."

"Not exactly," Alex said hesitantly.

"Huh?" Steven said. He and everyone else stopped eating and looked at Alex.

"I wouldn't go so far as to say that *no* relative of yours could help Marcie out," Alex said.

"Oh?" Steven said, looking puzzled. "Is there a rich aunt I don't know about?"

"No," Alex said, looking over his father's shoulder at the wall. "No rich aunt, Dad. But maybe a son who knows how to—how shall I put this?—handle money judiciously."

Two or three pieces of silverware could be heard falling onto plates. Simons and Marcie looked interested. Each of the Keatons looked astounded.

"Alex," Elyse said, "you have ten thousand dollars?"

"Well, not exactly ten thousand," Alex said, trying to minimize the effect of what he had just revealed.

"How much, exactly?" Steven asked.

"Ten thousand, six hundred, and fourteen dollars and seventy-six cents," Alex answered. "As of four P.M. today."

"What do you mean as of four P.M.?" asked Mallory.

"That's the time the stock market closes in New York," replied Alex. "I call my stockbroker every day after the market closes to check on my portfolio. I made a real killing today on wheat futures."

Alex looked from Mallory to Jennifer, then from Elyse to Steven. All four of them were staring as though he had grown a second nose.

"Come on," Alex said. "It isn't that amazing. I mean, you all knew I've been saving something every week for years."

"Yes," Elyse said, "but you've also been buying your own clothes since you were twelve."

"And his own razor blades since he was sixteen," Jennifer said.

"Even though he didn't start shaving for another year," Mallory added.

"Well, yeah," Alex said. "I've been sort of supporting myself for a while. But I've also been investing my funds. Moving small amounts in and out of money markets, picking up a mutual fund here, a certificate of deposit there. And, after all is said and done, I have a little bit more than Marcie needs."

"I think that's just amazing," Marcie said. "Elyse, would you object if I tried to convince Alex to buy a piece of my shop?"

"No, no," Elyse said distractedly. "Of course not."

"Steven?" Marcie asked.

Just as distracted as Elyse, Steven said, "No, go right ahead and make your pitch."

"Well," Simons said, "I for one hope Marcie can talk you into it, Alex. You have an astute business sense, and the two of you together would be bound to succeed."

"Nobody has to talk me into it," Alex said. "I've already decided to let you have the money, Marcie."

"Great," Jennifer said. "Now we can finish eating dinner."

"Our son the capitalist," Steven said, smiling at Elyse. "Who would have believed it possible?"

# CHAPTER
# 7

"Hey, guys!" Walt called out as he and Alex entered the Nu Alpha Mu house. "Gather round and listen to what Alex Keaton has been up to lately."

Alex had run into Walt after class, and they had walked to the house together. When Alex mentioned that Simons had been at his home the night before Walt pumped him for information. Alex felt as though he'd just been interviewed for a gossip magazine, and he was loving every second of the attention.

"This young man," Walt said, leading Alex into the living room, "had a couple of guests for dinner last night."

Alex, wearing a wide grin, allowed himself to be seated on a couch. Six or eight of his fraternity brothers surrounded him as Walt continued his announcement.

"The guests," Walt went on, "were none other than Professor Simons—and a date."

"No kidding!"

"I don't believe it!"

"With a date!"

"Now, now, gentlemen," Walt said, "quiet down, because there's more to tell."

The grin was plastered on Alex's face. He sat back on the couch with the air of a celebrity at a friendly press conference.

"Mr. Keaton," Walt said, "tells me that he and Simons's date got to talking about a business venture she plans to undertake. And guess who her new partner is going to be."

They all looked from Walt to Alex, who was now stretched out on the couch. The future titans of industry were in awe of their new brother. Their new brother beamed.

"What kind of business?" Ken asked. "You aren't going to drop out of school, are you, Keaton?"

"Drop out of school?" Alex said, laughing. "No, I'm not going to run the business. I'm just buying a piece of it. She needs some up-front capital, and I had a little idle cash lying around."

Mouths were beginning to drop open around him. So he decided to milk the situation for all it was worth.

"What kind of business?" Ken repeated.

In the best British accent he could muster, Alex answered, "We're going to operate a hairdressing salon."

"You're going to be a hairdresser?" Frank said.

"Correction," Walt said. "He's going to have hairdressers working for him. All he'll have to do is rake in the dough that the hairdressers make for him."

"Ahhh," Tim said dreamily, falling into a stuffed chair. "Making money without working. *That* is the name of the game."

"I wouldn't say I won't be working," Alex said. "I mean, I'll spend some time at the place when I can. Operate the cash register, check out the receipts, maybe test out a can of hair spray now and then."

"Checking out the receipts sounds like a good idea to me," Ken said. "If you're not going to be there, how do you know your partner won't pocket some cash once in a while?"

Alex wasn't grinning any more, and he sat up to look at Ken. "Why would she do a thing like that?" he asked.

"Are you kidding?" Lee said. "The question you want to ask is, Why *wouldn't* she do it? Come on, Alex, she's there with the day's receipts, and part of it belongs to you. All she has to do is slip a chunk of it into her pocket, and your share disappears. Who do you know who wouldn't take advantage of that situation?"

"I wouldn't," Alex said.

"Oh, I know," Lee said. "I meant present company excluded."

Alex realized that Lee didn't believe him. "I really wouldn't, Lee," he insisted.

"Maybe not," Walt said, "but how do you know your partner wouldn't?"

"I'll give her the benefit of the doubt," Alex said, uncomfortable with the turn the conversation had taken. "I mean, until I have reason to think otherwise, I might as well trust her. Right?"

"Yeah, I guess so," Ken said. "Just keep an eye on her. And get one of those cash registers that keeps a daily record of everything."

"Do you have an accountant for the business yet?" Frank asked.

"I don't know," Alex said. "This only happened last night, for Pete's sake. She probably has an accountant."

"Don't use her accountant, Keaton," Tim said. "If she's skimming money off the top, she's going to have an accountant who can cover it up for her."

"But nobody said she's going to be skimming money," Alex protested.

"Get your own accountant," Frank said. "I can put you in touch with my uncle, if you want. He's got a reputation for some pretty creative bookkeeping, especially when it comes to income tax."

"Listen, guys," Alex said, getting up from the couch. "I appreciate all this good advice. But it's just too soon for me to be worrying about problems. We don't even have a contract yet. I think for a while I'll just enjoy the *idea* of being a venture capitalist. When the reality arrives, I'll think about the possible problems."

He had removed himself from the center of the circle, and he now sat on a windowsill, staring out at the campus while he tried in vain to recapture the glow he had felt just a few minutes ago.

"He's right," Walt said. "Right now, it's just a kick. He can get responsibility later."

"Investing money is a serious business," said Ken.

"And I don't think it's ever too soon to worry about problems," added Frank.

The circle broke up, and they all went back to whatever they had been doing before Alex and Walt had come in. Walt sat in a chair near the window.

"Not to change the subject, Alex, old bean," he said, "but I had lunch with Nan Winters yesterday."

The mention of her name gave Alex a funny feeling in the back of his neck. He wondered if anything showed in his expression.

"Nan Winters?" he said. "How is she?"

"She's fine," Walt said. "You know, Nan and I are old friends."

"No, I didn't know that," Alex said.

"Oh, yeah. My parents have this summer place three houses away from her parents. So we go way back, Nan and I."

"How about that?" Alex said, wondering if

Walt were trying to lead into something.

"That's why Nan sometimes confides in me," he said.

"Really?" Alex said. "And did she confide in you yesterday?"

"She did indeed, young man," Walt said. "It seems the woman has a powerful crush on you."

"On me?" Alex gasped. His face turned red, and he added, "I don't believe it. Why, we hardly know each other."

"It's true, my friend. The woman is warm for your form. I think you should move immediately on this."

"What do you mean move?" Alex said. "You know I have a girlfriend."

"Oh, yes, there's Ellen," Walt said, nodding his head. "It's a pity. She's quite a girl."

"Yeah, I know she is," Alex said.

"I was talking about Nan," Walt said, picking up a magazine.

"Oh, yeah, well, I'm sure that she's quite a girl too," Alex added rather weakly.

# CHAPTER
# 8

"Is that you, Alex?" Mallory called into the kitchen from the living room.

"No," Alex answered. "It's Clint Eastwood. I've come to shoot your kitchen to bits."

"Come on in here," Jennifer called. "We were just talking about you."

In what seemed like a single fluid motion, Alex closed the door behind him, put his briefcase on the counter, opened the freezer door, took out an ice cream bar, took a bite, and went gliding into the living room. Then he spoke through a mouthful of ice cream.

"Vis muss be yr rucky day," he said.

Both his sisters, sitting on the floor in front of the TV, looked up at him.

"I suggest you swallow it and try again," Jennifer said.

He worked the ice cream around in his mouth, swallowed most of it, and said, "I said, this must be your lucky day."

"Why is that?" Mallory said without looking away from the TV. "Are you moving out?"

"Because you were talking about me," Alex said, "and I walked in the door. How many people can lay claim to such a fortunate coincidence? It so happens that I have just returned—"

"Shh! Wait!" Mallory said, holding her hand up to silence him and gaping at the TV.

Alex walked around to where he could see the screen. "Mallory," he said, "it's a dog food commercial!"

"Shh!" she hissed. "There's this great-looking guy in it. There he is!"

Alex fell onto the couch and took another bite of ice cream. When the commercial was over, Jennifer flipped the TV off and turned to Alex.

"You just returned from what?" she asked.

Alex's third bite consumed the rest of the ice cream bar. He held his hand up to signal Jennifer that he'd be right with her. Then he went to work on the ice cream in his mouth.

His sisters sat and watched as his face showed the effects of having put too much ice cream into his mouth.

"What a lovely sight," Jennifer said. "And me without my camera."

Alex finished his chewing chore and stood up. "I was about to say before that I've just returned from the lawyer's office. You are now in the presence of a man who owns ten percent of Shear Magic."

Jennifer and Mallory applauded, and Jennifer added as loud a whistle as she could come up with. Alex acknowledged the cheering with a deep bow.

"So it's really official now?" Mallory asked.

"That's right," Alex said. "I'm in the haircutting business."

"Alex," Jennifer said, "if you're in the business, you should at least get the name right. Barbers are in the haircutting business. You're in hairdressing."

"So what were you guys talking about before?"

"About Shear Magic," Mallory said. "What else? I was telling Jen that I've told everybody at school about Marcie and how great the place will be. All my friends promised they'll go there within the next two or three weeks."

"And I did the same thing," Jennifer said. "I don't know how Marcie is going to handle all the business she'll be getting."

"Hey, that's pretty good," Alex said. "I didn't know you guys were so worked up over this. I had the feeling nobody here really cared about it very much."

"Wrong-o, Alex," Mallory said. "Don't you realize what you're doing? You're in the very business I dream about going into myself someday."

"And *that* brings up my next point," Alex said.

"I have some good news for both of you."

The front door opened, and Steven came in. "Hi, everybody," he said cheerfully. "Mom home yet?"

"Not yet," Jennifer said. "She called a while ago. Should be home any minute now."

"How did things go at the lawyer's office, Alex?" he asked.

"Fine, Dad," Alex said.

"Alex," Mallory said, "what was the good news you were about to tell us?"

"Oh, yeah," Alex said. "After we left the lawyer, Marcie and I talked a little bit about how she plans to run the place. I suggested that we—that is, *she*—hire you guys to work part-time. And she said it was a great idea."

Mallory and Jennifer both shrieked with delight, jumped up, and tried to throw their arms around Alex. The force of their attack was too much for him, though, and he fell backward onto the couch. In their excitement they pursued him, but he slipped under them, crawled away, and stood up behind a stuffed chair.

"Easy, girls," he said. "Such displays of emotion are uncalled for. You may, if you like, come over and kiss my graduation ring. But you'll have plenty of chances to express your gratitude in the near future. I guarantee it."

Mallory looked over at Steven, who had been watching from the foot of the stairs. "Isn't that great, Dad?" she said.

"Yes, Mallory," he said quietly. "Yes, it's very good news."

Alex was puzzled by Steven's mild reaction. But before he could ask what was behind it, they heard Elyse's voice from the kitchen.

"Hi, honey. I'm home."

Jennifer and Mallory ran to talk to her. Steven followed, and Alex thought his father was avoiding eye contact with him. He followed Steven into the kitchen.

"—part-time jobs at Shear Magic!" Mallory was saying. "For both of us!"

"Isn't that terrific, Mom?" Jennifer said.

"Yes, it is," Elyse said, taking her coat off and draping it over a chair. "It really is terrific." Alex saw her share a glance with Steven, a glance that told him neither of them thought it was terrific at all.

"I have to call Denise and tell her about this," Jennifer said excitedly.

"I have to call everybody and tell them!" Mallory said, and they ran upstairs together.

Suddenly, the kitchen was very quiet. Both Elyse and Steven seemed ill-at-ease, and Alex watched them nervously moving about the kitchen, getting things ready for dinner.

"Dad?" he said. "What's going on? Mom?"

"Going on?" Steven said, taking a pot from a cabinet next to the stove. "The oven is going on. We're making dinner."

"Very funny," Alex said as he walked over and

took the pot from Steven, who offered no resistance. He put the pot on a counter, then gestured toward the table.

"Please sit down, Dad," he said. "You too, Mom."

They both eyed him as they sat at the kitchen table. He placed a chair between them and sat down.

Then he said, "Look, Mallory and Jennifer were too excited to notice, but I wasn't. When you heard about them working at Shear Magic, you both reacted as though they'd agreed to do my ironing for several years. There's something you two aren't telling me."

He waited, looking from Steven to Elyse, back and forth. Steven stared thoughtfully at the table. Elyse seemed ready to talk, but she was groping for the right words.

"Let me see if I can make it easier for you," Alex said. He got up from the chair and began to pace in front of the table. "Unless I miss my guess," he said, "your feelings about Shear Magic are something short of ecstatic."

He looked at Steven for confirmation. Steven seemed to be weighing Alex's last statement. Then he raised his eyebrows and nodded in agreement.

Alex looked at Elyse, who stared back at him for a few seconds. Then she, too, nodded.

"Okay," Alex said in the tone of someone determined to crack a puzzle. "Something short of ecstatic. Now, am I also correct in believing that this ecstasy shortfall extends to my involvement in Shear Magic?"

Both his parents nodded together. Alex stopped pacing and sat again in the chair between them.

"You didn't want me to put my money into the place?" he asked. "Why didn't you tell me that?"

"It isn't that we didn't want you to, honey," Elyse said. "We just had some reservations about it, that's all."

"And we didn't tell you about them," Steven said, "because we didn't want to discourage you in your first real business venture."

"But—" Alex stammered. "But you're my parents. I trust you. I appreciate hearing advice from you," he said, then added, "sometimes," to keep them from getting the wrong idea.

"And we're usually more than willing to give it to you, Alex," Elyse said. "But this time, we weren't so sure we were right."

"We're still not sure," Steven said.

"The suspense is going to kill me," Alex said. "You two better tell me what you're talking about."

Steven took a deep breath. Then he said, "Alex, when you came up with this idea at dinner two weeks ago, my first reaction was shock. I found it hard to deal with the fact that my son has more discretionary funds than I have."

"But, Dad, I explained to you."

"I know, I know," Steven said. "I was only telling you about my first reaction. Once I got past the shock, I began—*we* began—thinking about you running a business, or at least helping to run one."

"And we wondered if your sense of values might take a beating because of the business."

"What do you mean?" Alex asked.

"Oh, I don't know for sure," Elyse answered. "You know your father and I don't share your enthusiasm for business in general. We don't place as high a value on making money as you do. We've been worried that being a business-man—especially a successful one—might make you—well, the way you already are, only more so."

"And why didn't you tell me this before?"

"Because," Steven said, "we seem to be past the point where we can teach you anything you don't already know. And, besides, we're not certain that we have the right to try to force our attitudes about money, and business, and things like that on you."

Alex stood up and stepped away from the table. "Wow," he said softly, running a hand through his hair.

Elyse and Steven watched him resume pacing in front of the table. "Wow," he muttered again.

"Wow what, Alex?" Steven asked.

# Family Ties®

*Photo Album*

"My parents thought I might be making a mistake," he said. "But they didn't tell me because they thought *they* might be just as likely to be wrong. I say wow to that."

"I see what you mean," Steven said. He and Elyse both got up and walked to him.

"Now that you know what's been bothering us," Elyse said, "there's only one thing left to say."

"What's that?" Alex asked.

"Knock 'em dead with Shear Magic," she said. She kissed him on the cheek.

"Good luck, son," Steven said, hugging him.

"Thanks," Alex said. "Both of you." He took a deep breath, sighed, and walked toward the doorway.

He stopped at the door and spoke in his normal tone. "Boy, this emotional stuff is pretty draining. I'm glad we don't have many conversations like this one. I don't think I could handle more than one in, say, every eighteen years."

# CHAPTER
# 9

"Thank you very much, ma'am," Alex said. "Come back to Shear Magic soon." He gave her several singles in change, as a gentle reminder that she was expected to tip the people who had worked on her hair. Then he sat back and surveyed his domain.

Since this was Wednesday, four full-time hairdressers were busy with customers. On Fridays and Saturdays, two part-timers were added to the staff. Mallory was washing a fifth customer's hair while Jennifer swept the floor.

Customers were coming in at the rate of one every ten minutes or so. And every time one did, Alex mentally calculated the profit that was likely to be derived. It was this calculation that kept him smiling and cheerful whenever he was talking to a customer.

He swiveled the high stool to face out into the shopping mall. He couldn't imagine how Marcie might have picked a better location than this for a hairdressing salon. Not only had they developed a list of steady customers in a few short weeks, but they were getting a lot of referrals and walk-in business too. He felt as though he'd put his money into a gold mine.

He took care of another customer, added her profit contribution to the pile in his head, smiled, and hopped down from the stool to make his rounds. This consisted of a slow walk down the main aisle of the shop, a smile and a nod of the head for each customer, and an occasional instruction for one of the workers.

This trip his smiles were especially large, because he felt terrific about the day's profit-figure in his head. Halfway down the aisle on the way back to his stool, he noticed something under one of the chairs.

"Jennifer," he said pleasantly, "there's a bit of hair on the floor over there. Would you mind sweeping it up?"

"I'm going to straighten up the stockroom right now, Alex," Jennifer said. "I'll get that later."

She went to the back room, and Alex stood there with his pleasant smile glued in place. He forcefully reminded himself of where he was and of the presence of customers. With the smile still glued on, Alex bent down and picked up the hair himself. Then he slowly ambled back to his post at the front of the shop.

"Hi, Alex," Ellen said, walking in from the mall.

"Ellen!" he said brightly. "Hi! What are you doing here?"

"I needed to pick up some gift wrap on the way home. So I thought I'd get it in the mall and also get a chance to see you."

"I'm glad you did," he said. "I was thinking last night about how little we get to see each other these days, now that I'm spending so much time here."

"Where's Marcie?" she asked.

"She had some errands to run, and she asked me to watch over things. She should be back soon. Maybe we can have a soda together or something."

"I don't think so," she said. "I have a lot of studying to do. How's business?"

"It's great!" Alex said. "My share of today's profits will finance a dinner in the restaurant of your choice. Provided the restaurant of your choice is one of the inexpensive ones we usually frequent."

"Good," she said, laughing. "But maybe it would be better to bank your share of today's profit. As a hedge against recession, or some other unforeseen setback."

"Unforeseen setback?" he said, hopping onto his stool. "Are you kidding? I'm already planning expansion. If we keep up this rate of business, we should be able to open a second shop in less than a year. The third one would be only a year behind that. After that, I'll consider franchises.

Marcie and I could become the McDonald's of the hairdressing industry."

She smiled and shook her head. "What does Marcie think of all this?" she asked.

"Well, I haven't exactly discussed it with her yet," he said. "She has her hands full running this first place of ours. I want to give her a chance to get her bearings around here before I introduce her to the world of big business."

"Alex!" a girl's voice called from the mall. "Hey, Alex!"

Alex looked out, and Ellen turned to see Nan Winters walking toward them. She was carrying two shopping bags from one of the department stores in the mall. She walked up to the cash register and put the bags down.

"I was hoping to find you here," she said excitedly. "This is the third time I've stopped by."

Alex nervously glanced at Ellen, who was looking at Nan. "Yeah," he said, "well, I don't actually work here. I just sort of help out—"

"You just sort of own the place is what I've heard," she said, broadening her smile.

"Well," he said, swallowing hard, "I own a small piece of the business, yes. Nan Winters, this is Ellen Reed."

"How do you do," Nan said, smiling as sweetly as she knew how.

"Hello," Ellen said, smiling just as sweetly. No one was fooled for a second by the mutual sweetness.

"I think I'll go say hello to Mallory and Jennifer," Ellen said. "Nice to meet you, Nan." She walked briskly into the store.

"Walt told me all about your new business," Nan said. "I think it's really exciting."

"Well, yes, it is," Alex said, trying to watch Ellen as he spoke.

"And I understand Professor Simons is involved too."

"Only indirectly," he said, wondering if Ellen had noticed Nan's eyes. Of course she had, he reasoned. You'd have to be blind not to notice them.

"He's a friend of your partner's?"

"Yes. That's how this whole thing got off the ground. But he doesn't actually have anything to do with the business."

"Still," Nan said, "I think it's exciting that you're involved. I know that you'll be successful, and I hope you make a fortune on the place."

"Thanks," Alex said, smiling weakly.

"Well," Nan said, picking up her shopping bags, "gotta run. See you in class tomorrow, okay?"

"Yeah," Alex said, feeling relieved that she was going. "Yeah, see you tomorrow, Nan."

He went inside, where Ellen was talking with Mallory, who was between customers. "Hi," he said. Why was he feeling guilty?

"I was just leaving," Ellen said.

"She just stopped by to wish me luck," he said,

66

trying to make it sound as insignificant as possible.

"Who?" Ellen asked.

"Nan," he said. "Nan Winters."

"Oh, Nan," Ellen said. "And did she?"

"Did she what?"

"Wish you luck," Ellen said.

"Yes. Yes, she did."

"Good," Ellen said. "I have to go. See you tomorrow night."

"Right," Alex said as he watched her walk away.

"What was that all about?" Mallory asked.

"Nothing," Alex said, frowning.

Jennifer came out of the back room and said, "Alex, we just got a delivery of supplies, and somebody has to sign for it."

"I'll take care of it," he said.

In the stockroom he found a burly man waiting impatiently with an invoice to be signed. Alex took it from him and looked around for the supplies.

"Just sign it and let me out of here," the man said rudely.

"I'd like to check it against the delivery," Alex said.

"The blond already did that," the man sneered. "Just sign it, will you?"

"The blond happens to be my sister," Alex said angrily.

"Yeah, well, your sister happens to be a blond,"

the man said. "Now sign the thing and let me get going."

"Hey, do you know anything about courtesy?" Alex asked, his voice rising. "I'm going to call your company and let them know how you talk to customers!"

The man looked him in the eye and chuckled. "You do that," he said. "And if you don't get any satisfaction from them, maybe you can take your business elsewhere. But I don't think you will."

He laughed loudly at that, and Alex wondered why. Without checking the boxes the man had delivered, Alex signed the form and handed it to him. The man tore off one copy, held it out for Alex to grab, and walked away.

"What was that all about?" Alex said aloud. "And what the heck was so funny?"

# CHAPTER
# 10

"A business has to be run like a business," Alex proclaimed. "There's no place in business for sentiment, emotion . . . not even for family feeling. Pass the potatoes, please."

Elyse passed the potatoes, but said nothing. Steven, Mallory, Jennifer, and Ellen were all determined to do the same thing, but Alex was making it difficult.

"Just today," Alex said as he spooned mashed potatoes onto his plate, "I was telling Marcie how we have to apply cost accounting methods to everything we do. How each and every job has to be justified according to rigid standards. Dad, can I have the bread, please?"

"I really enjoy what I'm doing at the shop, Ellen," Mallory said, as though she hadn't heard a thing from Alex.

Ellen smiled at her. "It sure looked that way when I was there yesterday," she said.

"I never thought I could actually have fun

washing other people's hair," Mallory said.

"I suggested she install a time clock," Alex said. "No sense paying anyone for minutes not spent on the job."

"How about you, Jennifer?" Ellen said. "You seemed to be having fun there, too."

"Oh, yeah!" Jennifer said. "I get to talk to so many people everyday. And I don't work hard at all."

"Ineffective labor relations," Alex went on, "have been the cause of many a business failure. I don't intend to let that happen to my business venture. Tighten those screws, I say. Get everybody to put their nose to the grindstone!"

Steven spooned gravy onto his meat. Then he said, "It'd be pretty difficult for anyone to cut hair in that position, Alex."

"Just a figure of speech, Dad," Alex said after swallowing some food. "The point is, if you let your workers get the upper hand, you'll end up with no business. Then everybody is a loser—workers, owners, the whole lot."

"Well, dear," Elyse said. "It isn't as though you have to worry about production schedules and assembly lines, you know. Your workers are hairdressers, not mechanics."

"Doesn't matter, Mom. Good management of employees is a basic principle, no matter what type of work they're doing."

"Marcie told me one of the hairdressers might give me lessons soon," Mallory said, not paying the slightest attention to Alex's pronouncements.

"That's terrific," Ellen said.

"Yeah," Mallory said. "She said I might be able to give a customer a trim once in a while."

"Then maybe I can move up to washing," Jennifer said.

"It must be great to get paid for something you get a kick out of," Ellen said.

"You guys sound like you're talking about being at a rock concert, not working at a job. This is supposed to be serious. Who ever said you should have fun on the job?"

"Come on, Alex," Ellen said, poking him with her elbow. "You seem to be having fun when you're there."

"I'm the owner!" he said with a bit more feeling that the situation called for. "I put up the money for the place! Well, part of the money anyway. I'm supposed to enjoy it. That's what having money is all about."

"And what about the workers?" Jennifer asked. "Would you rather have everybody else unhappy? Is that what you want?"

"No, no, Jennifer," Alex said. He put his knife and fork down so he could explain himself more clearly.

"I want my workers to be happy. All we owners do. But I want them to be happy for the right reasons. Job satisfaction does not consist of having fun and talking to people. It comes from doing a job well. Tell me you're pleased because you swept that floor as well as it could possibly have been swept. Tell me that, and *then* I'll give your pleasure on the job my stamp of approval."

"Do we have any cream pies in the refrigerator?" Steven asked.

"No," Elyse said. "You know we're having ice cream for dessert."

"I wasn't thinking of dessert," Steven said. "I was thinking of what Alex just said. The only appropriate response I can come up with is to hit my son in the face with a cream pie."

The phone rang as Alex said, "Now, come on, Dad—"

"Your turn to get it, Alex," Mallory said as she reached for a slice of bread.

Alex made a face, got up and threw his napkin on his chair, and went to the kitchen to answer the phone as Mallory and Jennifer continued talking about how happy they were to be working at Shear Magic.

When Alex came back, he sat down in sulky silence. All eyes turned to him.

"Pass the salt, please," he said.

Elyse picked up the salt and passed it to him. "Who was on the phone, Alex?" she asked.

"It was Marcie."

"Really?" Steven said. "What did she want?"

"Oh, just some business she wanted to talk over," he said evasively.

"What sort of business?" Ellen asked.

Alex hesitated, annoyed at the questioning. Then he said, "Well, if you must know, she called to talk to Mallory and Jennifer. I told her I'd take a message."

"Yes," Mallory said. "And what was the message?"

"She said to tell you," Alex said slowly, "that several customers commented on how courteous and efficient you both are. She said to tell you that you're both doing a terrific job. And she also said she's glad to have the two of you working for her."

The short silence at the table was deceiving. When Alex looked around the table, he found he was completely surrounded by grins. He could almost hear the noise of the grins, and then everyone except Alex began to laugh.

"All right, so Marcie's pleased with them," he said. "I still say work should not be fun. If work and play were the same thing, why would we have two different words for them?"

He looked down and pretended to be intensely interested in what was left of his mashed potatoes.

# CHAPTER
# 11

"And so," Professor Simons said to his class, "it comes down to a question of who is responsible to whom—and of who is responsible *for* whom."

He nodded to a student in the back of the room who had her hand raised. Alex, who was sitting in a front seat, turned to look at her. As he did, Nan caught his eye and smiled at him.

"I'm not entirely sure of what you're saying, Professor," the girl in the back of the room said. "Do you mean that the standards of morality— or honesty, or ethics—are different for different groups in society?"

"Not at all," Simons said. "The standards remain fixed for all of us. What changes is—"

He stopped and looked at Alex, who was fidgeting in his seat. With a slight smile, he said to the girl in the back, "It's my guess that Mr. Keaton has something to say on the subject."

"Well, yes," Alex said, a little surprised. "As a matter of fact, I do."

He turned to face the class. He considered standing to address them, but decided against it. He cleared his throat and launched into his explanation.

"The difference," he began, "is in the way each group relates to society as a whole. Take the police, for example. Their relationship with the rest of us is one of protector. In that role, they're empowered to do things that we don't let others do—carry guns in public, arrest us, search our homes, and so on."

He could see Simons out of the corner of his eye, and he imagined that the professor was looking approvingly at him. He could see Nan straight on, however, and he didn't have to imagine anything. She was eyeing him with great admiration. On second thought, he decided, it was awe.

"Since each group has a different responsibility to society," he went on, "each group has to interpret the prevailing standards of ethics in its special way. That means that the leaders of industry are not necessarily expected to follow the rules in the same way as others. Sometimes this may mean sacrificing the interests of certain powerless groups to the good of society as a whole. But difficult decisions like that are among the burdens of leadership."

He couldn't have timed the bell any better if

he had written a script. It rang just as he finished, and the class quickly made its move toward the door. Alex wasn't surprised to see Nan hold back and wait for everyone else to leave.

"Nicely put, Alex," Simons said, putting his books and papers into his briefcase. "Of course, you've opened up a highly debatable area of discourse here. We'll pick up on it in our next session."

Simons walked out, and Nan came up and stood in front of Alex. "That was great!" she said, flashing her smile.

"Thanks," Alex said as casually as he could. "It felt pretty good being able to do it."

They walked out of the classroom together, Alex holding the door open for her. "Professor Simons seemed impressed," she said.

"Did he?" Alex asked. "I didn't really notice."

"Well, I did," she said. "He was beaming at you like a proud father."

"Well, he did seem to be glowing a bit," Alex said.

Nan stopped walking and faced him. She hesitated for a few seconds, then blurted out, "Alex, there's a sorority dance at school this Saturday. I was hoping you would come with me."

Something in him wanted to remind her about Ellen, but he was lost in her eyes. Was this gorgeous creature actually asking him—Alex P. Keaton—for a date? She was, indeed.

"I—uh—" he stammered.

"There isn't anyone I'd rather go with," she said in the most sugary voice he had ever heard outside of the movies.

He stared at her for a long time. Then he said weakly, "Sure. I'd love to go to the dance with you."

She leaned over and kissed him on the cheek. "Thanks," she said, then walked off down the hall.

He stood there watching her. Then he banged his head lightly against the wall behind him.

"Pain," he said. "That means I'm awake. Which means it really did happen."

Smiling, he took a deep breath and let it out slowly. Then the smile suddenly disappeared.

Saturday night, he thought. Ellen. Oh, no. What am I going to tell Ellen? I must be going crazy!

# CHAPTER
# 12

Several hours later, Alex was filling in for Marcie at Shear Magic. He had told her that she could take the afternoon off and that he would lock up at the end of the day. Three hairdressers were busy with customers, Mallory had just finished a washing, and Jennifer was straightening up at one of the empty stations. Alex walked slowly down the aisle on an inspection tour.

He leaned over to one of the working hairdressers and said in her ear, "Very nice, Alicia. Keep up the good work."

She stopped cutting to give him a surprised look, but he was already past her and examining the next station. At this chair, a hairdresser named Joanne was explaining to a customer the various styles that would complement her features.

Alex eavesdropped for a few seconds. Then, while the customer studied a magazine photo, he said out of the corner of his mouth, "Don't give her too many options, Joanne. We have a time schedule to concern ourselves with here."

Joanne looked at Alex with something less than friendship in her eyes. Before she could say anything, though, Alex was already moving on.

Alex saw Jennifer leafing through a magazine she had picked up from an empty seat. "Hop to it, Jen," he said, snapping his fingers. "This is a workplace, not a library."

"Cool it, Alex," she said without looking up from the magazine. "Marcie said it's all right for us to read, as long as there are no customers waiting to be served."

"Hmm," he said as he walked into the back room. Efficient inventory control was as important, he reasoned, as labor relations. Besides, the boxes in the back room never answered him back.

Several boxes of hair spray, shampoo, conditioner, and other supplies were in various parts of the room. He decided the space would be better used if he consolidated the boxes in one corner. At the same time, he could make an inventory list and talk to Marcie about what supplies had to be ordered.

He carried one box to the empty corner. Then he picked up a clipboard with a blank inventory sheet on it. He squatted to see what the box contained.

"That's funny," he said. The box had been stamped HAIR SPRAY. But it had no manufacturer's code number on it. And there was no ship-per's label.

He went over and looked at another box. It was stamped SHAMPOO, but it, too, was missing both a manufacturer's code and a shipping address. He checked a third and a fourth box and found the same thing.

He quickly ran through all the boxes—twenty or thirty of them—and found that none of them had the information he was looking for. By now, he had broken into a nervous sweat.

He moved to the other side of the room, where the hair dryers and other equipment were kept in boxes. He quickly surveyed these boxes and found what he already expected. All of them were missing manufacturers' codes and shipping addresses.

He was breathing heavily, and his shirt was damp with perspiration. He kept telling himself not to jump to conclusions, but he didn't see how he could avoid the obvious. Shear Magic had been buying stolen goods.

Wait till Marcie heard about this.

# CHAPTER
# 13

"I didn't mention it to Jennifer and Mallory," Alex said, "because I didn't want to upset them."

He and Ellen were sitting at the kitchen table. No one else was home, and he had just told Ellen about his discovery in the stockroom.

"Are you sure code numbers and shipping addresses are supposed to be on the boxes?" she asked.

"El," he said, "I've been handling the inventory ever since Marcie moved in. I'm the one who checked the stuff she took over from the previous owner. Trust me. I know what the boxes are supposed to look like."

"Yeah," Ellen said thoughtfully. "Still, it's a big leap from missing addresses to stolen goods, isn't it?"

"I'd like to agree with you," Alex said. "But I've been thinking about it for several hours now, and I haven't been able to come up with another explanation."

"Maybe the labels fell off," Ellen said lamely.

"Forty-seven of them?" he said. "Not very likely, wouldn't you say? Besides, I examined them. No glue, no tape marks. These boxes never had any shipping labels to begin with. That means—"

"I know, I know," she interrupted. "Stolen."

"But there's also the final piece of evidence, which I haven't even told you about yet."

"What's that?" she asked.

"Last week, I was filling in for Marcie when a shipment arrived. I went back to sign for it, and I ran into an ape straight out of a 1930s gangster movie. You should have seen this guy! No neck, no chin, and eyebrows like jungle brush. He had a voice like a wounded lion, and his biggest problem was keeping his knuckles from scraping the floor as he walked."

Ellen smiled at the description. "So what?" she asked. "What does all that have to do with your theory?"

"It's not a theory, it's a fact," he said quickly. "And I'd think the connection was obvious. This guy was exactly the type you'd expect to see in a hot-goods operation. He was ready-made for the part."

"I've probably heard sillier expressions of prejudice during the past five or six years," Ellen said, leaning back and folding her arms. "I just can't seem to think of one right now. Just because someone doesn't look like Robert Redford doesn't mean that he's a criminal."

"Maybe it is prejudice," he said. "But listen to this. I told this goon I was going to let his boss know how rude he had been to a customer. And he laughed at me."

"So?"

"Well, it wasn't so much that he was laughing," Alex said. "It was more what he said."

"What was that?"Ellen asked.

"He said something like, 'Go ahead and tell my boss. And if that doesn't work, maybe you can take your business elsewhere. But I don't think you will.' "

Ellen waited. Then she said, "So far, it doesn't sound very suspicious to me."

"No, no," Alex said, "you don't understand. The way he said it, he made it sound like the last thing in the world I'd consider doing. It was as though he and I were conspirators in something."

"Oh, I see," Ellen said. "And now you think it's because he knows you're not going to go to a competitor."

"Right!" Alex said. "Because, unless I'm wrong, he doesn't have any real competitors."

The phone rang, and Alex jumped up from his chair. "That's probably Marcie," he said. "I left a message on her answering machine."

He raced to the phone as Ellen went to the refrigerator. She took out a pitcher of orange juice and poured a glassful while he talked.

"Marcie," Alex said, "I stumbed on something disturbing this afternoon, and I wanted to let you know about it."

He paused for a few seconds, then went on. "I was moving boxes of supplies around, and I noticed that not one of them has a manufacturer's code or a shipping address. What does that mean? Well, I suspect it means there's something at least questionable about the stuff we've been buying."

Ellen had moved to where she could watch him as he listened to Marcie. As Marcie talked, Alex's face went through a series of reactions. He looked puzzled. Then his eyebrows shot up. Then he wrinkled his forehead in a scowl.

Finally, he said, "Well, yeah. Sure. I mean, if you say so. Yeah, I'll see you tomorrow, Marcie. Bye."

He hung up the phone after frowning at the receiver. He looked at Ellen, then walked slowly to the table, where he fell into a chair. He rested his chin on his hand and stared at the wall.

"Well?" Ellen said.

"Well," Alex said. "Well, I wish I knew what to make of that."

"What did she say?"

"Not much," he said. "She didn't seem at all concerned about it. In fact, she stopped me before I could even say the stuff might be stolen. She said she'd rather talk about it tomorrow. She said not to worry about shipping labels or

84

anything else, because supplies and equipment were her problem, not mine."

"Sounds like good advice to me," Ellen said. "Alex, there's probably a perfectly reasonable explanation for those boxes. You don't know how she orders the stuff, or who delivers it, or anything else. Why don't you let it rest until tomorrow. She'll explain it to you then."

"Yeah," he said unsurely. "I guess you're right."

"Which allows us," Ellen said, "to talk about much more important matters."

"Like what?" he asked, brightening a little.

"Like Saturday night," she said. "This is the first weekend in a month that I don't have to hole up with my books. What do you feel like doing?"

Alex was out of the chair again. "I can't believe I forgot to tell you," he said. He scrambled around the kitchen looking for something to hide his guilt-inflicted nervousness. He decided on the orange juice pitcher.

"Forgot to tell me what?" Ellen asked.

Pouring himself a glass of juice and keeping his back to her, Alex said, "About—uh—the economics club. Yeah, we're having an informal get-together Saturday."

"No kidding?" she said. "That's okay. I don't mind going with you."

He gulped down the juice and put the glass on the counter. "No, no," he said quickly, "you don't understand. When I say informal, I mean informal. Just a bunch of guys sitting around talking about international monetary policy. Over beers."

"Guys?" she said. "The economics club has female members too. One or two very noticeable ones, if memory serves me," she added in what Alex took as a direct reference to Nan Winters.

"Yes, yes, we do have girls in the club," he said. "But this get-together doesn't include any of them. This is a sort of eco stag party. No members of the fair sex have been invited."

She sat there smiling and shaking her head at his choice of words. "So I can't come along," she said.

"'Fraid not," Alex said, carefully avoiding looking at her. "You know if it were up to me . . ."

She sighed and said, "Well, it isn't the end of the world. Maybe I can get ahead on some of the reading I have to do for my poetry course."

She got up and walked over to the stove. "How about a cup of tea?" she asked.

He nodded and thought, Not the end of the world. The end of the world might be a little easier to deal with than what he was feeling right now.

## CHAPTER
# 14

"Believe me, Marcie, I have been trying to come up with another explanation, in fact, *any* other explanation that would cover the facts," said Alex. "I tried convincing myself that some manufacturer had come up with some miracle vanishing cream that automatically removes identification numbers. But even I couldn't buy that one."

They had just opened the store. One of the hairdressers was at work on a customer while Marcie and Alex talked in the back room. That is, Alex talked. So far Marcie had just listened, slowly walking around the room, pretending to be straightening up while he propounded his theory.

"I just can't shake the feeling that we're accepting deliveries of stolen goods," Alex finally managed to blurt out. "But," he quickly added,

"I'm confident that you, Marcie, had no idea that these possibly stolen goods were being delivered to the shop."

Alex let out a breath of air, which Marcie took as a signal that he was finished talking. For the first time since they had come into the room, she looked him full in the face. She let several seconds go by. Then she said, "Sit down, Alex."

A puzzled look came over his face. This wasn't the kind of reaction he was expecting. He sat on a low pile of boxes.

"Let's talk business for a few minutes," Marcie said. "Do you remember what our contract says?"

"Sure I do," Alex said, looking more puzzled. "But what has this got to do with what I've—"

"It has everything to do with it," Marcie said sharply. "You lent me ten thousand dollars. I have eighteen months to pay you back. Until I do, you get five percent of my monthly profit, as interest on the loan."

"I know what our financial arrangements are," Alex said impatiently. "I could recite the whole contract to you word for word. But what does that have to do with the goon and the funny deliveries?"

Marcie ignored his impatience and continued to speak slowly, deliberately, almost as though she were talking to a child. "You get five percent of the profits. The higher the profits, the more you make. Now, doesn't that give you an interest in seeing the business run as efficiently as possible?"

"Of course it does!" Alex said, raising his voice and standing to face her. "Why do you think I spend so much time here all week? Why do you think I'm always riding herd on the staff? The maximization of profits has always been among my highest ideals, but what does that have to do with our conversation?"

For several seconds, Marcie silently looked him in the eye. Then she turned and paced back and forth in front of him.

"You make your small contribution to the profit picture, Alex," she said, "but I make the lion's share," Marcie said pointedly. "Part of my contribution is to keep my expenses as low as possible. See those hair dryers over there? I got them at half price."

Alex looked over at the hair dryers in the corner as though he had never seen them before. He had no interest in seeing the pile of boxes. But he was also intent on avoiding eye contact with Marcie, now that he was beginning to understand what she was trying to explain to him.

"Some of the supplies in this room cost me less than a third of their normal prices," she said. "I've saved more money on these supplies than you've made from the place so far."

Alex was looking around the room, trying to pretend that the boxes were the most fascinating objects he'd ever laid eyes on. He'd do anything to keep from having to look at Marcie.

"I'm a businesswoman," Marcie continued, "not the district attorney. I look for the best deal that I can get, and I don't ask for a pedigree. In a nutshell, Alex," Marcie said, "the less I spend, the more you make. Do you want me to start spending more on supplies and equipment?"

"Well, now that you put it that way, not exactly," Alex mumbled weakly, examining one of the boxes in front of him.

"Do you want me to explain to you why the prices are so low?"

"Sorry I brought it up," Alex said, walking slowly toward the door. "I'm confident that you have everything under control."

He walked out into the store in a daze, strode to the front, and perched himself on the stool near the cash register. He reached under the counter for a textbook, opened it, and pretended to be absorbed in its contents.

An hour later, he was still staring at the same page when Ellen came by for him. As soon as he saw her approaching, he slammed the book shut, hopped off the stool, and called out to Marcie, who was talking with a customer near the rear of the store.

"Gotta go, Marcie. See you on Monday!"

He hurried out and intercepted Ellen before she reached the entrance. "Hi," he said, kissing her on the cheek and gently steering her back out into the mall.

"Hi, yourself," she said, taken aback by his abruptness. "Where are we going?"

"Going?" he said absentmindedly. He glanced over his shoulder as though he suspected Marcie might be following them.

"Going?" he repeated. "Oh, nowhere. I just thought we'd walk around the mall for a while before we went to school."

"That's okay with me," Ellen said. "But I thought you had to work in the store this morning."

"Work?" he asked. "In the store?" He realized that he was beginning to sound like someone who was just learning the English language and not doing particularly well. He decided if he didn't calm down he might start hyperventilating right in the middle of the mall.

"Yes," he said, after doing some quick deep breathing exercises while Ellen stared confusedly at him. "You're right. I was supposed to work this morning. But I asked Marcie if I could leave so we could—uh—have some time to walk around the mall."

She looked over at him, and her mouth showed a tiny trace of a smile. "That was really sweet, Alex. Underneath that banker's three-piece suit you're really a pretty romantic guy, you know?"

"Look!" he said, pointing to a window display in a shoe store. "They've got those new Italian models. Latest thing in fashionable footwear."

He took Ellen's hand and led her to the shoe store window. "Nifty, don't you think?" he said, studying the shoes in the display with the intensity that he usually reserved for the Wall Street reports.

"Did you talk to Marcie?" Ellen prodded him.

"What?" he said, still pretending to be fascinated by the shoes.

"Marcie," Ellen said, walking slowly away from the shoe store. "Did you talk to her about the supply stuff?"

"Supplies?" he said weakly, as though he didn't recognize the word. "Oh, you mean about the back room and all that silliness. Yeah, I talked to her. Turns out it's no problem at all." He was looking around the mall like a tourist who had just wandered into Disneyland without a tour map.

Ellen stopped walking and took his arm, forcing him to face her. "What do you mean, no problem?" she asked.

"Huh?" he said. "Oh. It's just that you were right. I was making a whole big deal out of nothing at all. It was like you said. The boxes probably came from a distributor who removes the shipping labels before delivering the goods. Something to do with the way he keeps his records or something. Anyway, I'm just the investor, it's really up to Marcie to see that the store runs smoothly and—and profitably."

Alex could feel his face reddening, so he turned

and began walking again. Ellen, looking puzzled, fell into step with him.

"So," she said unsurely, "there was nothing to be concerned about?"

"No," he snapped. "No problems whatsoever."

"And you're satisfied with the explanation she gave you?"

"Absolutely," Alex said, his gaze once again wandering over the mall he had seen a thousand times before. "One hundred percent satisfied," he added for emphasis.

He turned and looked at Ellen. Her expression told him that his cover-up attempt was falling short of total success. To hide his panic, he grinned at her.

"Let's go have some hot chocolate," he said. "I'll bet you'd love a nice hot cup of hot chocolate right now."

He took Ellen's hand and led her toward the coffee shop. Ellen went along, but she was troubled by the way Alex was behaving.

# CHAPTER
# 15

Alex made one final mirror-check before leaving his room for the dance Saturday night. "Smashing," he said, grinning at himself in the mirror. "Positively smashing, even if I do say so myself."

He gave the knot of his tie a gentle tug, winked at his reflection, left the room, and bounded down the stairs. His parents were in the living room; Elyse was doing a crossword puzzle and Steven was reading a book.

"Car keys, Dad?" he said. Both parents turned to look at him just as Jennifer walked in from the kitchen.

"They're on the counter in the kitchen," Elyse said. "Didn't you say Ellen was busy tonight?"

"Uh, yeah," Alex said. He made a move toward the kitchen and bumped into Jennifer. The two of them then made three of four attempts to get out of each other's way, but they ended up where they had started. Jennifer laughed. Alex looked frazzled.

"Why are you all dressed up?" Steven asked.

"Dad, I'm not dressed up. Dressed up is a tux or a morning coat. I always wear a jacket and tie. You know that."

Jennifer, backing away and holding her hand to her nose, said, "Yeah, but you don't always try to take your life by drowning in a vat of after-shave lotion. Phew!"

"Where are you off to, Alex?" Steven asked. Both he and Elyse noticed that Alex hesitated a second before answering.

"Uh," he said, "a lecture at the frat house."

"A lecture?" Elyse said, putting her puzzle down on the coffee table. "On Saturday night?"

"Well, it's kind of special," Alex said, edging his way toward the kitchen. "It'll be followed by refreshments and all. It's kind of a lecture/party, sort of. I sure wish I didn't have to go. But the economics club put it together, and I'm kind of obligated."

He disappeared into the kitchen. Steven and Elyse shared a glance that suggested more than a little doubt over what Alex had just told them.

Jennifer asked, "Did he sound as silly as I think he did?"

"Thanks for letting me use the car," Alex called from the kitchen. "Don't wait up. I'll be home late." They heard the kitchen door close behind him.

Twenty minutes later, he stood at the front door of Nan Winters's house. "Hello," he said to the woman who opened the door. "I'm Alex Keaton. Nan and I are going to the dance together tonight."

"Come in, please," she said cheerfully. "I'm Mrs. Winters, and this is Mr. Winters."

Alex stepped inside and shook hands with Nan's father. "Pleased to meet you, sir," he said.

"A pleasure to meet you, young man," Mr. Winters said. "Come in and sit down. Nan said she'll be down in a few minutes."

Alex followed them into the living room, where they all sat down. Alex's eye was caught by a print on the far wall.

"Hey, that's Winslow Homer, isn't it?" he said.

"Yes, it is," Mr. Winters said. "Nan tells us you've recently been inducted into Nu Alpha Mu."

"Uh, yes, that's right," Alex said. "I took a course in American painters last semester. Homer is one of my favorite artists."

Mrs. Winters said, "We have a high regard for anyone who is accepted into NAM. It's an outstanding fraternity. Some of the most successful men in the country are NAM men."

"Yes," Alex said politely. "You know, I noticed a coin book on a table out in the hall. I used to collect coins when I was a kid."

"When I was in college," Mr. Winters said, completely ignoring Alex's attempts at conversation, "Nu Alpha Mu was the only fraternity I wanted to join. When they didn't accept me, I decided to stay away from frats altogether."

"Really?" Alex said. "It meant that much to you, huh? Where did you go to college, sir?"

"You're a very fortunate young man," Mrs. Winters said. "NAM is going to help you move quickly in the business world."

It was obvious that Nu Alpha Mu was the only thing these people wanted to talk about. Alex found himself getting annoyed that they didn't want to know anything about him—except the fact that he belonged to NAM.

That annoyed him, but the annoyance passed when he saw Nan coming down the stairs, and he looked up to see the vision he'd be spending the evening with. He swallowed hard to keep from gasping. Even at this distance, the sparkle in her eyes lit up the room.

"I can't believe you'd have trouble seeing the difference," Alex said in exasperation. He was talking to Brett Tarnell, the date of one of Nan's sorority sisters. Nan had a firm grasp of Alex's left arm and seemed to be hanging just as tightly on every word he said.

"There is no difference," Brett said. "If a welfare check is a government handout, then so is an income tax deduction."

"Now listen to me, Brett," Alex said in his most condescending tone. "Income tax deductions are intended to give a boost to those people who contribute to the good of society. Tax loopholes are our government's way of saying thank you to the citizens who create jobs for everyone else."

"It's a case of government helping those who need it least," Brett said testily.

"Oh, yeah?" Alex said, on the verge of getting angry. He kept his temper, though, and managed to think of a retort.

"Well," he said with a slightly nasty edge, "the Lord helps those who help themselves. And so does a Republican administration."

He turned to walk away from Brett, and Nan turned along with him. He could feel her grip on his arm tighten a little, and he knew, without looking, that she was gazing at him admiringly.

A few minutes later, while Nan was helping with the refreshments, Alex was confronted by Stan Gropius, a tall, pipe-smoking senior he had always found a bit hard to take. Stan held his pipe in his left hand and extended his right hand to Alex. Alex reached out timidly and shook Stan's hand.

"Congratulations!" Stan said heartily. "I heard that little debate you had back there with Tarnell. Made mincemeat out of him."

"Thanks," Alex said, trying hard not to laugh at Stan. "I guess I did get off a good one there at the end."

"My father owns a factory in Akron," Stan said. "And he has a string of accountants who can bend and twist the tax laws to fit almost any situation."

"You don't say," Alex said uncomfortably.

"Oh, yeah," Stan went on. "Without them, he'd be paying twice as much tax as he does. And, the way we figure it, that extra money would end up in the pockets of the so-called needy. And then where would we find anyone willing to work for the minimum wage, huh?"

Stan's conspiratorial wink made Alex cringe. "Where indeed," he said, edging away from Stan. "Got to find my date. Nice talking to you."

He stood on his toes and tried to find Nan's head among the dozens that bobbed up and down in front of him. When he saw Professor Simons coming out of the kitchen, he quickly made his way in that direction.

"Hi, Professor," Alex said. "I didn't know you'd be here."

"Hello, Alex," Simons said taking a sip of his drink. "It was a last-minute thing. Professor Davis is the faculty adviser here, and she asked me just this afternoon to come with her tonight."

"I'm glad she did," Alex said. "There's something I want to talk to you about."

Simons made his way to a corner where there were two empty folding chairs. He and Alex sat down, and Simons sipped his drink.

"What did you want to talk about?"

"It's about Shear Magic," Alex said.

"Ah, yes, I hear it's going well. When I saw Marcie last week, she was very happy about the place."

"Yeah," Alex said, hesitating. "Yeah, the numbers do look pretty good. But . . ."

Simons waited for several seconds, looking concerned. Then he said, "But what, Alex?"

"Well," Alex said, "I discovered—let's say an irregularity—the other day." Simons tensed up a bit and looked interested, so Alex went on more boldly. "All the stuff in the back room at the store is in unmarked boxes, and I figured that was a little suspicious. So I talked to Marcie about it, and I kind of hinted that she might be buying stolen goods without knowing it, of course, and, well, she was unconcerned about this possibly serious problem."

Simons sat back in his chair, the tension gone. He sipped his drink and looked at Alex for what seemed a long time.

"Don't you see?" Alex blurted out. "We're probably buying hot goods. And Marcie knows they're hot!"

Simons put his glass on a table next to his chair. He stood up, and Alex stood along with him.

"First of all, Alex," he said, "let me say that I don't know anything about how Marcie runs her business. She insists on doing it on her own, and I don't interfere. Then let me say that I'm a little surprised at you. Marcie has a good sense of business, which is why I believed that an investment in Shear Magic was a good idea. I thought you had the same kind of business

100

sense, but I may have been wrong. Marcie is using every means to keep her expenses low and her profits high. That's what business is all about, Alex."

Alex felt as though he'd just been kicked in the stomach. "Even if it means stealing?" he said weakly.

"Marcie hasn't stolen anything," Simons said. "She has bought supplies from a distributor. She is under no obligation to look into activities of companies that make deliveries to her shop."

"I guess not," Alex said, almost in a whisper. "I guess I was making too big a deal out of this, huh?"

"Yes, you were, Alex," Simons said, smiling. "Now what do you say we enjoy the party?"

He gave Alex a friendly pat on the shoulder and made his way into the crowd. As Alex stared after him, he felt a hand close around his.

"Hi," Nan said. "I was looking all over for you."

"Hi," he said glumly.

"What's the matter?" she asked. "Is anything wrong?"

He sighed and looked into her eyes. "Yeah," he said. "Listen, I hope you won't be too upset about this, but I don't feel very well. Do you mind if I take you home right now?"

# CHAPTER
# 16

Alex slipped the key from the lock in the kitchen door, closed the door gently, and quietly made his way into the living room. By the flickering light of the TV, he could see his parents on the couch, both asleep in their bathrobes. He walked over to the TV.

The instant he switched it off, Elyse sat bolt upright and opened her eyes. "Hello, dear," she said mechanically. "What time is it?"

"A little after twelve," he said.

Steven sat up and switched on a table lamp next to the couch. "Twelve?" he said groggily. "Isn't that a little early to be getting home from your lecture-slash-party?"

"Hmm," Alex said, reluctant to do any more lying for the evening. "Were you guys waiting up for me, or what?"

"Us?" Elyse said, pretending to be surprised at the question. "No, of course not. We were just anxious to see the two A.M. rerun of the ten o'clock news. Just in case we missed something the first time around."

"We were waiting up for you," Steven said. "Ellen was here at about nine o'clock."

Alex's mouth dropped open. "Ellen was here?" he said dumbly. "What for?"

"It seems she didn't think that there really was a lecture tonight," Elyse said. "She had the crazy notion that you were out with another girl."

Alex sat on the arm of a stuffed chair and stared at his feet. "I was," he said. His parents showed no surprise.

"She left this for you," Steven said, holding out a sealed envelope.

Alex took it and tore it open. He read the note silently.

*Alex:*

*I don't know if I'm madder because you lied to me or because you thought I was so stupid I wouldn't find out. The saddest thing, though, is that you lied to me. I hope you're ashamed of yourself. Please don't call me. I don't want to hear from you.*

*Ellen*

He folded the note and put it into his shirt pocket. Then he slid from the arm into the chair and slouched down as far as he could.

"What did she say?" Steven asked.

"She said not to call her," Alex answered. "None of the rest of it matters."

"Did she say never to call her again?" Elyse asked.

Alex took the note from his pocket and looked it over. "No," he said.

"Well, then, maybe you'll be really lucky, and somehow Ellen will be able to forgive your dishonesty," his mother said in a voice that showed that she cared for Alex but was angry at him for the hurt he had caused Ellen.

"You'll have to give her a little time to get over the pain," Steven said. "But I'm sure she'll talk to you again. Let's just hope she can find a way to forgive you."

"You really think so?" Alex said, brightening a little.

"Of course!" Elyse said, trying to sound cheerful. "Just give her some time."

"When did she leave the note?" Alex asked.

"About three hours ago," Steven said.

"You think it's too soon to call her now?" Alex asked, jumping up from the chair.

"Alex!" Steven said sharply. "Sit, Alex!" Alex fell back into the chair.

"You don't want to rush it," Elyse said. "Give it at least a couple of days."

"Do you want to tell us what's going on, Alex?" Steven asked.

"What's going on," Alex said, "is that I've been behaving like a jackass."

"Oh, darn," Steven said. "I thought we'd be getting some news."

"No, Dad," Alex said seriously. "I mean I've really done it this time. I can't believe how stupid I've been." He stood and faced them and said, "I just spent several hours with a girl who is beautiful and intelligent and who shares my fascination with business in general and with economics in particular."

His parents stared up at him as he paused for emphasis. "Yes," Elyse said, looking confused, "I can see how you must feel like a genuine fool."

"No, Mom, you don't understand. I mean, I let myself be distracted by those things. Nan may be interested in economics, but she couldn't care less about me."

"Then why did she go out with you?" Elyse asked.

"Nu Alpha Mu," Alex said, falling back into the chair.

Steven said, "You aren't going to spell the answer out for us in Greek, are you?"

"She asked me out because I was accepted by Nu Alpha Mu," Alex said. "That's all she cares about. That's all her parents wanted to talk to me about. They're a lot more concerned about my future prospects in business than about— well, about anything else."

"So," Steven said, "they've reduced you to a symbol, eh? Instead of Alex P. Keaton, they see a dollar sign."

Alex sat up and looked at him. "Very good, Dad," he said. "I couldn't have said it better myself."

"You couldn't even have said it as well," Elyse pointed out. "Otherwise, you would have thought of that on your own."

Alex winced as though he had been smacked in the face.

"I guess you're right," he said. "It's funny, you know. Although I dislike saying anything negative about the dollar, which is after all the backbone of the world economy, I've got to admit that having yourself reduced to a thing, anything, is not a very nice feeling."

"You never did tell us why you're home so early," Elyse said.

"Oh, yeah," Alex said. "Well, in the first place, I wasn't crazy about the party. I found myself talking with a guy who would probably trade his aged grandmother for a crisp new dollar bill. And the two of us were on the *same* side of the argument I'd just been involved in. That didn't make me feel too great."

His parents chuckled. Then Steven said, "That doesn't sound bad enough to get you home at midnight, though."

"No," Alex said thoughtfully, " it wasn't. What really drove me out of the place was a little talk I had with Professor Simons."

He began tentatively. Then he backed up and told them about his discovery in the store, about

Ellen's reaction to what he had found, and about his conversation with Marcie. He admitted that he'd let Marcie talk him into accepting something he knew was wrong.

"But I couldn't really accept it," he said. "I needed somebody to help me make sense of it all. So I decided to ask Professor Simons what he thought about it."

"And what did he say?" Elyse asked.

"Just about the same thing Marcie did," Alex said sadly. "I was really disappointed. In fact, I was floored."

Steven got up and sat on the arm of Alex's chair. He put his arm on his son's shoulder. "Alex," he said, "I was afraid something like this might happen. We both were. We just weren't quite sure what to do to keep you from getting hurt."

"Do you know what really hurts the most?" Alex said sadly.

Elyse shook her head.

"What really hurts the most," said Alex, staring down at the carpeting, "is that I really hurt Ellen and might have destroyed our relationship."

Elyse came over and knelt in front of Alex. "I know you like to think of yourself as hard-headed," she said. "Even cold-blooded. But you aren't really that way, you know."

"I try," Alex said. "Lord knows I try."

"No one will deny that, Alex," Steven said.

"I'd say you're going to have to rethink a few things," Elyse said. "Don't you agree?"

"Yes," Alex said, climbing out of the chair. He walked toward the stairway. "In the morning. Right now, my head feels like the inside of an overloaded clothes dryer."

He walked up the first few steps, then turned and faced them. "Hey. Thanks, you guys," he said. They both waved and smiled, and he went upstairs.

He undressed quickly, slid under the covers, and turned out his light. *Rethink a few things,* his mother had said. Should he have invested in Shear Magic? Should he have risked everything with Ellen just to go out with Nan Winters? Was Nu Alpha Mu really the frat for him? And what about Professor Simons?

Rethink a few things! He wished that he could apply for a permit to start all over again. No, he thought as he drifted off to sleep. He couldn't bear going through fifth grade with Mrs. Liotta a second time.

# CHAPTER
# 17

"Good morning," Mallory said as she came into the kitchen. "Hear from Ellen last night?"

Alex sat at the table and stared into his cup of tea. "Nope," he said.

He had spent all day Sunday reaching for the phone and hanging it up before he could dial Ellen's number. *I don't want to hear from you,* her note had said. On the other hand, as his mother had pointed out, it hadn't said *forever.* He finally decided to let Sunday go by and to try talking to her in person today.

Jennifer came in and said, "Morning. Leave the cereal out, Mal. Did Ellen call, Alex?"

Alex continued to stare at his tea. Mallory shook her head in answer to Jennifer's question. Mallory sat opposite Alex at the table while Jennifer poured a bowl of cereal. Steven came in, smiling.

"Morning, everyone," he said cheerily. "Did—"

"No!" Mallory and Jennifer said at the same time.

Steven looked at Alex, who was still staring. He started to say something, thought better of it, and went to the refrigerator to pour a glass of orange juice. Elyse came in.

"Good morning," she called. She opened her mouth to say something else.

Steven, Jennifer, and Mallory all cried "No!" at the same time, and Elyse looked wide-eyed at them.

Steven walked over to her and whispered, "Ellen didn't call." She nodded.

Alex stirred from his chair, took a small sip of tea, and put the cup down. He picked up his books and mumbled, "See you later." Then he walked slowly out the back door.

At nine-thirty, he planted himself in a doorway just inside the entrance to the humanities building, where Ellen had a ten o'clock class. He wouldn't have believed it was possible, but he felt even worse than he had earlier.

He'd spent the last half hour in the student lounge with three of his frat brothers. Alex had casually brought up a situation involving "a friend" who ran a stationery store. This friend, he told them, had a chance to buy material from a less-than-reputable supplier, who might even be dealing in stolen goods.

"Only a fool would pass up an opportunity like that!" was one reaction.

Another was, "What's good for business is good for the whole community."

The one that bothered him most was, "Those of us who take the risks and fuel the economic engine are entitled to bend the rules a little."

Alex was getting tired of hearing these anything-goes arguments, but he stayed cool during the conversation. He said he'd pass the opinions on to his friend.

He was about to go out into the parking lot and look for Ellen's car when he saw her coming up the walk. He waited for her to get inside the building. Then he stepped out from the doorway and jumped in front of her.

She stopped. Her face turned red and her eyes widened. She opened her mouth to speak.

Then her mouth closed and her eyes narrowed. She stepped to her left and began walking again.

"Ellen!" Alex said. "Ellen, please talk to me!" Ellen just kept walking so he raced in front of her. "Will you please listen to me?" he asked meekly. "One more sprint like that and I won't have any breath left to talk."

"Go ahead," she said stonily. She was trying to make a face as hard as her voice, but it wasn't working. Alex fought hard against the urge to reach out and touch her cheek.

"Ellen," he said, "you're making a mountain out of a molehill. This girl Nan from my eco class is taken with me. You of all people should appreciate that. Well, she asked me the other day—"

Ellen stepped to her left and was walking off again. "Wait!" Alex yelled.

He ran to her, stood in front of her, and tossed his books aside. Then he put both hands on her arms to stop her.

"I'm sorry, Ellen!" he said desperately. "That was dumb. I'm just so afraid of losing you. Please listen to me."

She waited a long time, staring into his eyes the whole while. Finally, she said, "Okay. Talk to me." Alex sighed and let her arms go. He bent down and picked up his books, and they walked slowly down the hall.

"I'm not exactly sure how to begin," said Alex tentatively. "I know I've made a mess of things and behaved like a fool."

"That seems like an excellent starting point," Ellen said sharply.

"Look, I know that going out with Nan wasn't only wrong, it was stupid. She doesn't mean anything to me, and I certainly don't mean anything to her."

"And when did you discover that?" Ellen asked, looking straight ahead.

"I've kind of known it all along," Alex said. "But I guess I chose to ignore it. I guess it was more fun pretending that I was as attractive and smart as Nan told me I was."

Ellen looked at him but did not say anything.

"But the truth is that she didn't even know who I really was," he said. "She was impressed by the fact that Professor Simons singles me out in class all the time. And even more impressed that I had a business deal that involved him. So were the guys in the fraternity, for that matter. It just seems like all of them were impressed by something other than *me.*"

He stopped walking and took her arm. "I also realized that no matter what, you've always cared more about me, not about what frat I belong to, or what my teachers think of me, or what color tie I wear."

"Did you realize anything else?" Ellen asked in an even voice.

"Yes, I did," Alex replied. "I learned that losing you would be the worst thing that could ever happen to me."

"Nicely put," Ellen said as she leaned over and kissed his cheek.

"I'm sorry," he whispered.

"Accepted," she said, smiling. Then the smile disappeared, and she added, "But don't ever let it happen again. I wouldn't know how to forgive you if you ever lied to me again."

"I'll never give you the opportunity," Alex replied as he hugged her.

Later as they walked through the shopping mall, Ellen asked, "How late will you be working?"

"I don't know for sure," Alex said. "Come with me and we'll find out. Then I want to take you out for a candlelight dinner."

"Well, I hope your folks have candles in the house, because they've already invited me to dinner."

When they reached the shop, they saw Joanne cutting one customer's hair while another customer sat reading a magazine. Ellen followed Alex into the store.

"Hi, Joanne," Alex said. "Marcie here?"

"No," Joanne answered. "She's at the bank. Said she'd be right back. Mallory and Jennifer are in the back."

As they approached the back room, they could hear a man's voice, louder than Alex would have liked, with customers up front. He and Ellen stepped into the back room, and she closed the door behind her.

"Just take the pen in your pretty little hand," the man said gruffly to Mallory, "and let me get a move on. I got six more stops to make today."

Alex recognized him as the same delivery man he had argued with two weeks earlier, and he felt anger rising up inside himself. He stepped between the man and Mallory.

"I see you've dropped by for your regular courtesy call," Alex said.

It took a couple of seconds, but the man finally recognized Alex. "Oh," he said sarcastically, "it's little Mr. Sunshine. Now, I know you *are* allowed to sign for this, because you did it last time."

"I won't sign for your delivery," Alex said, "and neither of my sisters will either. So maybe you should just—"

"They're both your sisters, huh?" the man said. "Well, then, I guess I better be careful what I say."

"Don't say anything," Alex said, his voice rising. "Just get out."

"Not until I have a signature," the man said.

"Nobody's going to sign that paper for you," Alex yelled as the door flew open and Marcie rushed in.

"What's going on in here?" she hissed in a stage whisper, closing the door behind her.

"Oh, Marcie," Alex said. "Good. You're just in time for the Shampoo Connection. This gorilla—" The man took a step in Alex's direction, but Marcie got between them. "That's enough, Alex," she said.

"No, it isn't!" Alex said hotly. "This guy insulted me! He insulted my sisters! And he's probably ready to insult Ellen!"

"Alex!" Mallory said. "Stop it! You sound like an idiot!"

"Listen to her," Marcie said calmly. "She speaks the truth."

"Don't you tell me about the truth!" Alex said. The floodgates opened, and he let everything come pouring out.

"The truth! The truth is that this guy is delivering hot goods! The truth is that you know very well where this stuff is coming from. And it's the truth that Professor Simons"—his voice cracked

115

a little there—"knows all about it too! Don't tell me about the truth! I wouldn't be surprised if you guys are into gunrunning and smuggling also!" By now, he was screaming. *You're probably getting your backing from some Communist dictatorship in South America!"*

The only thing that stopped him was that he ran out of breath. The words stopped, and he stood there, redfaced and panting. The room was absolutely silent, except for the distant hum of the hair dryer Joanne was operating.

Mallory and Jennifer looked at each other as Marcie backed away from Alex. Ellen walked over and put her hand on his arm. This seemed to startle him back to reality.

He looked sheepishly from his sisters to Marcie, to the deliveryman, and then to Ellen. After about ten seconds of silence, even Alex was embarrassed at his exaggerated outburst.

He strutted to the door. At least, he intended it as strutting. To everyone else in the room, it looked like a clumsy attempt at tap dancing. He put his hand on the doorknob and spoke in a higher pitch than he would have liked.

"Marcie," he said, "I think there's a form there that needs your signature."

He slipped out the door while the rest of them remained wide-eyed and frozen in place.

# CHAPTER
# 18

"I'll get it!" Alex hollered. He hopped off the couch and bounded to the front door. He opened it to find Ellen smiling at him.

"Hi," he said and leaned forward and kissed her. "Hi," she said. She stepped inside, and he closed the door and led her into the living room. They both sat on the couch.

"Dinner will be ready in a few minutes," he said. "Listen, I'm really sorry about that blowup this afternoon. In fact, if you don't want to stay for dinner, I'll understand."

"Stop talking like a jerk," she said. "After what you told me this morning, I can understand the explosion. I just wish you had talked to me about all of it earlier. You shouldn't have kept it from me." "I know," Alex said. "That's part of what I feel sorry about. I've really been acting like an idiot. I just hope you can forgive and forget."

"Forgive?" she said. "Consider it done. Forget? Well, that's something else again. I'm not

117

sure I ever want to forget that show you gave this afternoon." She laughed, and Alex hid his face in his hands.

Jennifer came in from the kitchen. "Hi, Ellen," she said. "I'm taking orders for dinner drinks."

"I'll have water, please," Ellen said.

"How about you, Silver Tongue? Will you have time to drink? Or are you going to spend the evening denouncing the forces of evil throughout the world?"

"Cola, please," Alex said, his head still in his hands.

"Hello, Ellen," Mallory said, coming down from her bedroom. "I wasn't sure you'd be here tonight."

"Why not?" Ellen asked.

"Oh, I don't know," Mallory said. "Sometimes I wonder exactly how much embarrassment you'll allow my brother to put you through. But whenever I think about it, I always realize the truth."

"What's that?" Ellen asked, laughing.

"That if you're going out with him in the first place, you must be ready for a life filled with embarrassing moments."

Steven and Elyse came into the living room. "I'm letting the roast cool a little before I slice it," Steven said. "We'll be eating soon."

"Is that okay, Alex?" Jennifer asked nervously. Then she turned to her parents and said, "Don't rub him the wrong way. Once he gets annoyed, there's no telling what he might do."

"No matter how stupid it sounds," Mallory added.

"All right," Elyse said, laughing along with everyone else. "That's enough. What do you say we just lay off Alex about this afternoon?"

"Oh, okay," Mallory said grudgingly.

"Well, maybe just for half an hour," Steven said.

"No," Elyse insisted. "No more. Alex lost control this afternoon. Sure, he said some silly things. In fact, he made a fool of himself. Maybe he even acted like an idiot."

"Mom," Alex said, "if this is your idea of defending me, I wish you'd join the opposition."

"He said some things he'd like to take back," Elyse said. "We've all done that at one time or another." She paused, then added, "Though I don't think any of us could ever top his performance."

"As your one and only father," Steven said, "sorry, Alex, but it's true. I have only one regret—that I couldn't be there to witness the momentous event."

"Oh, Dad," Mallory said excitedly, "you should have seen it. There was Alex, babbling on about guns and smugglers—"

"Enough!" Alex cried. "I admit—out loud—that I made a monkey of myself. I have never behaved as foolishly as I did for one brief spurt this afternoon. But are you going to punish me for the rest of my life for a single moment of stupidity?"

"Of course not, Alex," Steven said.

"But can we have the rest of the night?" Jennifer asked hopefully.

Elyse abruptly changed the tone of the conversation. "Alex," she said, "have you decided what you'll do about your investment?"

"The decision is really up to Marcie," Alex said. "Once she pays me back my money—with interest, of course—I no longer have a share in her company. I have a feeling she'll pay me back pretty quickly."

"Well," Steven said, "I'm glad you got out this easily. I was afraid you might have to get burned before you learned a lesson."

"No burns, Dad," Alex said, holding out his hands for display. "A couple of stings, maybe, but no burns."

"Any lessons?" Elyse asked.

Alex looked thoughtful. Then he said, "Yeah, I think so. I learned that some people think the rules weren't meant for them."

"And?" Steven asked.

"And . . . they're wrong," Alex said. "The rules are either for all of us, or they're for none of us."

"So I guess this means you won't be having much to do with business any more," Mallory said.

"Why not?" Alex asked.

"I don't know," Mallory said unsurely. "You

said Marcie deals with shady characters. Professor Simons seems to approve. You were complaining before about all your fraternity brothers having the same kind of attitude."

Alex looked at Mallory, surprised that his sister could be so sharp. He didn't say anything for a while.

"Well?" Elyse said. "What about that, Alex?"

"All those things are true, Mallory," Alex said. "Except not *all* my frat brothers are like that. Most of them, but not all. But I figure it this way. Maybe a lot of people in business do have a set of ethics that make me cringe. But that's no reason to stay away from business. In fact, it's a good reason to get into it. Somebody has to teach them the right way."

"Attaboy, Alex," Steven said. "Come on, Elyse, let's get dinner out before Alex really gets rolling and the roast gets cold."

Elyse and Steven left the room. Mallory, Jennifer, and Ellen stared at Alex. He stood up and took a deep breath, clearly pleased with himself.

"Alex?" Jennifer said.

"Yes, Jennifer?"

"Does this mean you're going to have—a conscience or something from now on?"

"Something like that," he answered, giving his attention to making some last-minute adjustments to the table setting.

"Will you be making more speeches like the

one you gave this afternoon?" Ellen asked.

"Possibly," he said, still intent on the table. "One never knows when a situation will arise that calls for a superior moral sense."

Ellen and his sisters were now directly behind him, though he didn't realize it.

"And, Alex," Mallory said softly, "can we expect you to sound off whenever one of those situations arises?"

"You can count on it," he announced.

He turned just in time to see the three of them pounce on him with sofa pillows. He fell to the floor screaming as the pillows—first Ellen's, then Mallory's, then Jennifer's hit him in rotation over and over.

Steven and Elyse walked in and saw him smothered by the three pillows.

"Good children," Elyse said.

"As long as they don't fight," Steven said, stepping over them and putting the roast on the table.